Last Wish of Summer

by

Phillip Overton

Strategic Book Publishing and Rights Co.

Strategic Book Publishing and Rights Co.
12620 FM 1960, Suite A4-507
Houston, TX 77065
www.sbpra.com

ISBN: 978-1-61204-296-1

For my children
Rochelle and Brandon
May all your wishes come true

Acknowledgements

A story comes together in many ways, and this book would not have been possible without the help of the many people who have been persistent in their encouragement of me writing it. Firstly to my wife Denise for partnering with me on life's adventure, I thank you from the bottom of my heart for the hours spent listening to my continually evolving ideas. The depth of character that shines through on the following pages I attribute to you, for remaining radiant in your support through any storm that passes by. To the inspiration I find in my daughter Rochelle's creative wisdom and my son Brandon's strength of character, I thank you both. This book is for you. Thanks to my mother Barbara, my sister Debbie, Richard, Phillip and Kerryn, for your continued and often excited enquiries as to how my next book was progressing. Your excitement is contagious. To my sister Tanya and her husband Luke, I thank you both for being such great supporters. It was your turn Tanya to have a character named after you in this book. To the entire staff at Strategic Book Group, thank you for believing in the success of this book. Thanks also to my growing band of readers, and those I am sure will join with me in the support of this book in the coming years. To Pastor Dan O'Farrell, your advice forever changed my outlook on life. Finally to God the Father, thank you for not giving up on me. A lot of years have passed since I first dreamed of writing a novel at the age of nine, and you have been with me every step of the way. I hope you will be proud of my attempt to use your gift to shine the glory back on you.

prologue

utomobiles aren't supposed to crash into sandcastles. Yet that is exactly what happened every year on the night before Tanya Sorenson's birthday. Her parent's silver Toyota would come crashing through the timber barriers at the end of the parking lot and out onto the sand. Kicking up clouds of sand in the headlights as it bounced across the beach, until finally it skidded to a halt and slammed hood-first into a perfectly formed sandcastle just above the high water line.

She would then listen as the radiator hissed in protest. It's slow ticking noise acting as a countdown to the moment she knew would follow. Without the ability to run over to the vehicle and drag her parents out, she could only wait while her screams were lost somewhere in a silent vacuum.

On cue, the horn would blast, and, as if from nowhere, the semi-trailer would appear from the milky pre-dawn darkness and slam into the side of the vehicle at high speed. There was no way the occupants could have survived a crash of that magnitude.

Then Tanya would wake up. It was all just a dream. Tanya reminded herself of this, but that fact did little to comfort her. Her parents were really gone.

Tanya swung her feet over the side of the bed and sat up. Her toes wiggled into her pink, fluffy slippers and instinctively she made her way to the kitchen. Her puppy lifted its head from where it lay curled up at the foot of her bed and thought better than to follow. Choosing to watch instead as her master shuffled past the open window before disappearing into the darkness of the apartment.

Reaching the kitchen Tanya poured a juice and stood in the light of the open refrigerator door. The cool air danced across her clammy skin and felt just as refreshing as the drink itself. It was another of those sticky hot summer nights that made it hard to get a good night's sleep. The dream only ensured that tonight would be even more difficult.

Leaving the empty glass on the kitchen counter, Tanya shuffled back through the small apartment and stopped when she reached her bedroom window. In the still of the night the sound of the ocean floated in easily through the open window, accompanied by the faint smell of salt air. It was the reason why she chose to sleep with the window open. Closing it would mean having to listen instead to the noisy drone of the twenty year old air-conditioner.

Neatly kicking off her slippers she climbed back into bed and nestled her head on her pillow while staring blankly at the ceiling. Why did she continue to have this dream? Tonight had made the third year in a row that she had woken just as the big rig had slammed into the side of her parents' Toyota. Wasn't it hard enough for a daughter to live with the grief of losing both her parents in a car accident without having to dream about the crash in all its detail? And why in her dreams did it always have to take place on the beach? Her parents had died at an intersection in the city. The beach was her one place of solitude. Her happy place she went to whenever she felt sad and alone. So why was God allowing two worlds to collide like this in her dreams, and always on the day before her birthday? Was there some detail she was missing? She wished she knew.

The curtains caught her eye as they moved a little. It was the first sign of any breeze so far tonight. Perhaps she could ask Him. Maybe He knew the answers to all the questions that were going through her mind. Wait a minute. What was she thinking? Of course He knew the answers, after all He is God. And God as anyone will tell you is supposed to know everything. Right?

So why did God allow her parents to die in the accident? Not only was it a good question, but it was the same question she came up with every time she thought about the accident in detail. Normally it was also the point that she would give up thinking about it and go do something else to get her mind off the subject. She'd try to remind herself that it was just their time. When God says your time is up. Then your time is up. And there was nothing more anyone could do about it.

Tanya closed her eyes. When she opened them again nothing had changed. The curtains were still blowing ever so softly in the breeze and deep down she was still angry. Yet somewhere deep inside she found the courage to finally push aside the unanswered questions. And she began to pray.

"Dear Father, I know You are up there watching over me and I know You have the answers to all of my questions. I know I can't expect You to whisper to me the words I want to hear on the early morning breeze. But just because I can't see the wind doesn't mean that it isn't there. I only notice it when it reveals itself, like right now as it is blowing through my curtains. Lord I know the answers to my questions are somewhere I can't see right now. But I'm tired of struggling to know why You have taken away from me the ones I have loved most in my life and I'm tired of feeling more lost every time I come to You in prayer. Although I'm sorry that it seems to be less often these days. I'm supposed to be a Christian. I'm supposed to find comfort in your presence. But I feel it less and less each day because this thing is eating me up. I don't want to go on like this. I want You to fill my life again with dreams. Yet what is the point of having dreams if they bring you no comfort?"

Tanya stopped praying as she let out a yawn. Suddenly her eyes were feeling sore and tired, and she rubbed them once before continuing.

"I don't want to give up on going to church Lord, but ever since the accident I feel that I'm only there to receive everyone's pity. I feel that people must be thinking, 'Look at poor Tanya. It was such a tragedy for her to lose her parents the way she did. Her Faith must be so strong to have pulled her through such a difficult time.' Well the truth is that it isn't. I feel like I'm holding on to my Faith only to honor the memory of my parents. It isn't supposed to be like that. Only I don't know what I'm doing wrong. Please help me to feel close to you again God. You are all I have left. Actually I do have my dog Pookie, but that's beside the point."

At the sound of Tanya's voice the little dog bounded from the end of her bed and snuggled up close to her, licking under her chin. Tanya wrapped her arm around Pookie to keep her still while she finished praying.

"I know that You love me God and sent your Son to die for my sins. So forgive me if this prayer seems a little too forward. Please let me feel the love again that Jesus spoke of in the Bible. Ever since You took my parents away it's been missing in my life. I don't want to go through life alone and feeling this way. Please mend my brokenness..."

Tanya stopped to let another yawn escape.

"Heal my loneliness..."

She rubbed her eyes.

"Forgive my sins..."

And fell fast asleep.

She didn't get the chance to finish her prayer with an Amen. But God heard it anyway. It was the prayer He had been waiting three years for her to make. The curtains by the window became still once more, and Tanya lay sleeping peacefully with her little dog curled up in her arms in the small apartment she had occupied since moving away from the city.

Little did she know that God was about to do something special in her life.

Welcome to Kings Beach

3.00pm

I Need a Holiday

The door to the tiny sales office swung open, letting in a gust of stifling afternoon breeze that rustled the paperwork on Sebastian Wolsey's desk. In the confusion that followed, Ben Moore, real estate extraordinaire, strode out of his office to greet the customer. Descending on the slim thirty-something woman who had sheepishly walked through the front of the tiny real estate office while looking bemused at the sight of Sebastian grabbing at sheets of paper as they flew through the air.

"Good afternoon Ma'am. Ben Moore, King's Court Realty, how is it that I can be of service to you today?" He waffled as he straightened his neck tie. "Apartment, house or ocean views, I'm sure I have whatever it is you are looking for."

The lady took a moment to take in all the movement that was occurring in the tiny but well presented sales office before answering, "I'm sorry, all I was after was a rental list."

"Not a problem." Ben immediately turned the notch down on his full frontal sales assault on the lady who stood like a deer caught in the headlights on an oncoming car. Then trying his best not to sound disappointed, he stepped aside and with one hand motioned towards the desk tucked away in the front corner of the office. "I'm sure our letting agent Sebastian Wolsey will be able to help you. He's also our resident novelist, perhaps you've read one of his books."

The woman stood awkwardly in the middle of the room, glancing between the enigmatic Ben and the dark haired man perched behind the desk now clutching pages of whatever had been flying through the air only moments before.

"Sorry, never heard of him," she said absently.

"That's okay, not everyone has." Ben smiled and turned back towards his office.

Sebastian tried to conceal the glare on his face that was aimed solely at his co-worker who loved nothing better than to bring him down a peg or two at every opportunity. Instead he tried to smile valiantly at the now confused woman who stood before him.

"Here we are Ma'am," he said as he held his outstretched arm over the desk. "Here is a full list of this week's available rental properties in town."

"Thank you," she said as she stepped cautiously forward and accepted the sheet of paper that was dangling across the desk.

"If there's anything I can do to be of service..." he trailed off, but it was of no use. The door opened once more and she was gone.

Sebastian found himself once more grabbing at sheets of paper that he had only just returned to his desk from the last gust of wind the woman had invited inside. Now much to Ben's delight he found himself repeating his earlier performance. Only this time it was also for the benefit of none other than Walter Fry. Walter was the owner of King's Court Realty, a small yet successful real estate, property rental and holiday letting business in sunny Kings Beach. He was fifty, fat and right now he looked down right fearful.

"What's all this?" He mumbled as he stepped out from the confines of his cozy office. "Are we running a business here or are we conducting some kind of circus that I'm not privy to?"

"I'm sorry Walter. It's a bit windy outside," Sebastian apologized. "Some woman just walked in from off the street while I was tidying some paperwork and caught me by surprise."

"Organization Sebastian is the key to a successful real estate salesman," he began. "How many times have I stressed that we have to be ready the minute a customer walks in the door? If they see us up to our eyeballs in paperwork, they might just presume we haven't the time for them and take their business elsewhere."

For Walter to become involved in the day to day activities of the sales office was one thing, but for him to pry himself away from the sanctuary of his office was another thing all together. Unless it was for the purpose of shuffling across the road to the betting agency to place a bet on the greyhounds. Doing so usually indicated that he had lost money on the afternoon's horse races and was trying to win it back by throwing his money to the dogs.

"Sorry Walter, it won't happen again."

"That's all right, just see to it that you have whatever it is you are doing tidied up before you finish for the day," he said more calmly as he strode towards the front entrance. "I'll be back in a minute, there's a few dogs I fancy in tonight's races."

Sebastian watched the gray haired man as he opened the door and commanded his large frame to follow his legs which were all too eager to get to the betting agency before it closed. Only this time he was prepared for the late summer's wind which raced in once more through the open door, preventing an encore for the benefit of Ben who was watching smugly from behind the glass wall of his office. Finally the door closed and the small office returned to its normal state.

"So you didn't even get a chance to try and sell her a copy of your book?" Ben shouted from the other end of the building. "That's a shame."

Sebastian tried to ignore him. After all, it only fueled the desire for Ben to poke fun at him if he took his bait.

"If it's any consolation she didn't look like much of a reader," he continued. "It didn't take long for her to get bored talking to you, so imagine what she would have thought of your book."

"Give it a rest Ben," Sebastian snapped. "I've got enough to take care of here before the day is out without having to worry about you."

"Hey I'm only having a joke with you."

"Yeah, well it kind of loses its humor when you hear it for the millionth time."

"Whatever." Ben tried to hose down the serious element the repartee had taken. "Besides, I don't know why you won't accept the old guy's offer to sit the real estate exam and get your license. It would surely beat what you're doing now."

"My job suits me just fine the way it is," Sebastian explained, exactly as he had countless times before. "I need the regular hours and guaranteed income, and to do the course would interfere with my writing."

"Yeah but that obviously isn't working out for you so why pass up the chance to become a fully fledged real estate salesman instead of sitting at a desk all day handing out rental lists and taking holiday bookings? Think of all the commission you could be making."

"I'm fine," Sebastian answered, and the words seemed to hang in the air indefinitely, bringing the conversation to an end when in fact Sebastian was anything but fine.

The job was what it was. Hardly the aspiring choice of profession for a former bestselling author, far from an inspiring setting for a book and, undeniably difficult to deal with the two characters who seemed intent on reminding him of the fact at every opportunity. The one thing it did offer was that it paid the bills. Somewhere along the way he had become financially overcommitted. Soon after moving from a modest suburban home in the city to a brand new spacious home by the sea, the money from his first book had dried up. Shortly afterwards his second book was released, declared a flop and his contract with his publisher terminated. There was no more money.

The silence put everything into perspective for Sebastian. There was no point arguing with someone whose opinion counted for zero anyway. Besides, he knew as much as anyone that his next book could turn it all back around for him, if he could only get around to finishing it. For now he could at least try to be content that it was actually a good thing to let some time pass after the release of *Swimming with Mermaids*. A book which one reviewer described as difficult to forget, a sloppy, ill-conceived piece of trash that sticks in your mind long after you've convinced yourself to put it down. Although disappointment on a scale that grand was difficult to bounce back from, Sebastian had long ago convinced himself that it was possible. He believed he had another book in him every ounce as good as *Road to Nowhere*. One day he would be back on the bestseller lists and the Bens and Walters of this world could go jump in the lake. Only instead of taking solace in the thought, he actually felt like he was on a road to nowhere, quietly disappearing into oblivion behind a small desk in the corner of a little realtor's office in Kings Beach. There were dreams, and then there was the cold, stark nightmare of reality that seemed to prevent him from realizing any of them.

Then he thought of Tanya, and that made him smile. Tonight he was finally taking the pretty young waitress on a date. The fact that she was twelve years younger than him had only made it more of a challenge to finally convince the twenty-six year old that going to dinner was not abandoning the virginal Christian qualities she tried desperately to hide behind. Although he was sure there really was no halo to be found above her golden blonde hair and that it was merely a ploy to keep any potential male suitors at bay. The thought of being with her was one of the reasons he had been putting off planning his trip to Alaska for so long. The other reason was of course money.

"Any phone calls while I was gone?" Walter barked as he entered through the front door and Sebastian instinctively placed his hands over the pile of now neatly organized property agreements.

"No Walter. The phones have been dead all afternoon," Sebastian answered as he shook his thoughts back to the present.

"Good." He seemed curiously satisfied with the information and Sebastian couldn't quite put his finger on what didn't seem normal about his response.

"That gives us the rest of the afternoon to go over some of the finer points of recognizing what a potential client is looking for in a house," Walter said proudly. "Follow me to my office Sebastian, I think it's time you learnt a few pointers about the property market. It's safe to say that you won't be going anywhere soon with your books. So you may as well learn something while you're here."

'Oh please God,' Sebastian thought to himself. 'I could sure do with that holiday right now, and Alaska would be so much cooler than the stifling heat of a long hot summer in Kings Beach.'

3.30pm

Kings Beach Holiday Park

The blue urinal cakes always smelled better than the pink ones. At least that's what Anton thought as he finished his business and strode out of the orange brick amenities block of the King's Beach Holiday Park. The heat outside was stifling, and the asphalt beneath his bare feet even more so. Maybe by the time his friend Johnno got home from work the afternoon heat would be replaced by a cool breeze blowing in from the ocean. Strong enough to bring the late summer's temperature down from a staggering one hundred degrees Fahrenheit, but not so strong that it would flatten the afternoon swell. He always went surfing in the afternoon with Johnno. There was usually nothing else he had to do during the day, and he had no intention of changing that either.

For the likes of him he couldn't understand why anyone would want to work in heat like this. Actually Anton couldn't understand why anyone would want to work at all. He had successfully managed to avoid holding down a job for any longer than a day from the moment he had dropped out of high school halfway through his senior year. Work was merely a contributor to commercialism, a socio-economic disaster that should be cut off at the roots. In a world where big companies screamed at consumers to buy the latest and greatest, Anton simply didn't buy into it. Those who did always seemed to end up working long and hard for the privilege. Those who didn't seemed to rarely have anything worth worrying about in life.

Anton unzipped the faded annex on the aging mobile home nestled under a tree and stepped into its cool shade. The two old pedestal fans that he had bought for a song at a yard sale last winter had worked admirably all day. Along with the windows that were all open on the sixteen foot trailer home they had succeeded in keeping the temperature inside to an almost tolerable eighty-four degrees. Perfect he thought for lounging around without a shirt on and inventing new ways of generally doing nothing. And by the time he had turned twenty-five, he'd almost perfected it.

Surfing was best left for the mornings and afternoons. When the wind conditions were just right and the swell picked up on an incoming or outgoing tide. During the rest of the day you had to find something else to do to stop yourself from going mad. Otherwise you may as well find a Monday to Friday job like everyone else and start the cycle of counting down the days to the weekend.

Anton had tried working once or twice just to see if he liked the idea of actually doing something. The truth was he didn't like conforming to the ideals of a company run by some corporate suit trying to hide their personal problems by generally making life miserable for everyone else. The problem with bringing this to his or her attention was that they only seemed to want to rant and rave and shove you out the front door faster than you could say 'what gives dude?' Especially if you happened to laugh at the sight of them trying to maintain a professional appearance when all he or she wanted to do was jump up and down and scream at you to get out. So if you could make do with living off unemployment benefits, then it made more sense to collect your fortnightly benefit check and leave the corporate do-gooders to wallow in the pleasure of their own adulation. Even

9

if it meant that you had to prove that you were actively looking for work.

Anton sat down at the small table in his kitchen and pulled out the newspaper like he did every second Tuesday. Not today's paper mind you, but last Saturday's. Why pay for Saturday's newspaper when you could fetch it out of the garbage for free on Sunday morning? Especially when you were only applying for a job you didn't have any intention of ever getting anyway.

Taking out a lined, letter sized notepad, he quickly thumbed through the employment section until he found two job vacancies that seemed perfect for the task, and began to write using his messiest handwriting;

Dear Mr Man,

I saw your job in the paper the other day and thought I might have a go at it. I never knew the Kings Beach Council was lookin' for a Civil Engineer. I dunno what one is to tell the truth but it sure does sound interesting. I'm guessing it has sumpthin' to do with trains 'cause of the Engineer bit in your advert. I've always wanted to drive a locomotive and I think I'd make a real good Civil Engineer because when I was young I had a train set. I used to put two trains on the one track and watch them have a head-on crash! But hey, I understand that if I get the job I won't be allowed to do that anymore so you don't have to worry. I didn't know Kings Beach even had a railroad line so you'll have to tell me how to get there. Unless of course all you have in mind is one of those stupid kiddies shopping center train rides in which case you can forget it, I'm not interested!

Yours and all the rest

Anton
Xoxoxo

Once Anton had finished writing the letter and was satisfied that even he wouldn't employ himself if he was the last person on earth, he boiled the water to make himself a fresh cup of coffee. Even on a hot summer's afternoon the coffee smelled great as he poured the water in the mug and carefully added the milk and sugar. Then carrying the mug carefully to the small kitchen table, he placed it down roughly on top of the letter he had just written. The coffee splashed over the lip of the mug and spilled down the side, leaving a huge coffee ring on the newly finished letter.

"There, the Anton seal of approval," he said aloud for his own benefit.

3.35pm

Workin' for a Living

By the end of the day even the most hardened of construction workers had grown sick of the smell of concrete dust lingering in the air. John Clark had enough gray boogers in his nose to mold a small snowman, just as soon as he had the chance to blow the concrete hardened snot out of his nostrils. From the moment he had stepped on site at around seven this morning it was all he had been able to smell.

Tucked away in the stairwells of what was going to be a twelve story luxury apartment complex overlooking Kings Beach, he had done nothing but drill holes into the concrete floor of the stairwell all day. Even with the painters finally out of the way, the amount of tradesman passing up and down the stairs, carelessly flinging the doors open and almost sending him hurtling down the concrete steps was enough to drive him insane. Back here he was the forgotten worker, just another laborer to trip over on the way to the next floor.

While electricians, carpenters and plumbers all came and went about their business, he had the rather inglorious task of fitting door stops behind the stair doors. Not just a few doors, but every door on every floor that fed into one of the three separate stairwells in the building. Tomorrow would be the same only this time it would be the apartments themselves, starting at the bottom and working his way to the top. Much like his career actually, if one could call being a builder's laborer a career. His parents certainly didn't, but he didn't care. The money was good.

"Hey Johnno!" One of his workmates called out above the thud of the drill as it hammered its way through the concrete. "What are you doing? It's after half past, better get the tools down to the site foreman before he gives you a blast."

"Yeah. In a minute. I'm just finishing this last door," Johnno shouted back to him.

Only his parents called him John. 'John Clark,' they'd say. 'You should be back home in the city and studying at University instead of living by the beach, working on a construction site, surfing, drinking and practicing to be a bum.' To everyone else he was simply Johnno.

"Hey I'm talking to you! Haven't you finished those stairs yet?" The older laborer barked at him like he was his subordinate. "The boss is going to go nuts when you get down. He thinks you've already started on the apartments."

"Why would he think that?" Johnno panicked as he rushed to finish screwing the last door stop to the floor.

"I told him you should have finished the stairs by lunch," the older guy smirked. "Better lift your game tomorrow Johnno."

Johnno watched him walk away, his smug steps disappearing down the hall. Arrogance fitted him well. Johnno didn't know the guy's name but he didn't care. He was trouble in anyone's language.

The drill drove the last two screws into the plastic lugs he'd just finished tapping into the holes in the floor and he gathered his tools quickly as he got to his feet. Before he had time to sneeze another wad of concrete boogers from his nose, he was already bounding down the second flight of stairs. Finding his way to the basement, he raced over to the lockup beside the site foreman's office and dropped the drill and toolbox onto the workbench where he'd got them from early this morning.

"How's it going Johnno?" One of the other laborers greeted him as he turned to exit the small storeroom in the basement that was being used to lock up all of the company tools when not in use. "Feels good to be signing off for the day doesn't it?"

"It sure does mate," Johnno replied. "I'll be hitting the surf as soon as I'm out of here!"

"By the way, the site foreman was looking for you before."

"Are you sure?"

"Yep, passed him up on level four."

"What does he want?"

"I'm not sure. But I wouldn't even think about waiting around for him," the other guy joked. "If it was important he would have come looking for you before half past three."

"Yeah, you're right. See you tomorrow."

So with thoughts already turning to lines of clear blue waves lined up offshore for as far as the eye could see, Johnno brushed any further thoughts of work aside, and in his absent mindedness walked out. Straight past the tool register he was supposed to sign when returning any company issued tools. Straight past the time book he usually signed each afternoon to indicate that he'd left the site, and out into the wide blue yonder of an inviting summer's afternoon.

3.50pm

Anton's Caravan of Dreams

A nton barely even had time to bring the hot coffee to his lips before a shout at the door had him slopping a few more drops onto his second freshly written letter.

"Are you in there Anton? Let's hit the surf mate."

Anton got to his feet and brushed past the small table, poking his head out of the door to be greeted by the sight of his friend Johnno dressed only in his board shorts. Johnno was a stocky, well built, no nonsense kind of guy. A laborer for a construction company, he looked like the kind of guy you wanted on your side in a fight. He stood there giving Anton an impatient stare with those piercing brown eyes and matching hair that he simply wore pushed forward. Probably because his hair spent eight hours a day shoved underneath a hard hat.

"Do I have to say it again? Are you ready? Let's go."

"In a second dude." Anton smiled as he stuck his head back inside. "Just let me stick some stamps on these letters so I can drop them in the mailbox on the way."

"What? You've been home all day and you're only doing this now?" Johnno shook his head in disbelief. "Honestly mate, I don't know what you do with yourself all day."

"I keep busy," the reply came from within.

15

"Busy doing what?"

"You know, writing, dreaming, enjoying life."

"Yeah right I almost forgot the poetry thing." Johnno shook his head in quiet frustration. "Surely that can't keep you busy for an entire day, I mean how long does it take to write a poem?"

"If you dream a little, you'll have little to write about..."

"Yeah, yeah, I know," Johnno cut him off mid-sentence like he'd heard the line a thousand times before.

"If you dream a lot, you'll have writers' cramp," they both finished the sentence in unison.

"Well I wish you'd hurry up. I've heard that the surf's really pumping," Johnno snapped at him.

A moment later Anton stepped down into the annex and slammed the door shut behind him, wearing the same faded red board shorts and a tattered white Billabong singlet that he wore most days. He locked the door and turned to face Johnno, blue eyes dancing whimsically from beneath the scruffy dark blonde hair that hung across his forehead.

"All right my most righteous brother of the ocean, it's time to wet our feet and our souls in the sweet sea of life." Anton raised his hand to high-five his friend who rather than protest, lamely responded with a light, half-hearted slap of the palm.

Johnno shook his head in amusement and simply smiled as he always did when something profound erupted from his friend's mouth. Anton might be taller than him, but that didn't stop his lanky frame from appearing boney and lean whenever they stood together. Only Anton's innate ability to string together a perfectly good sentence on a second's notice made Johnno feel inferior in any way to his best friend. Someone had once told them they were the next generation odd couple. The truth was, apart from when Johnno went to work, they were inseparable.

"You finished now? Can we go?" Johnno joked with him.

Anton smiled as he brushed past him to pick up his surfboard which had stood solemnly all day in the corner of the annex. Picking it up under his arm he followed him outside into the glare of the afternoon sun. Johnno already had his surfboard packed neatly in the back of the blue and white Volkswagen Kombi that sat parked half off the road and half on the little asphalt roadway that sliced down the middle of the holiday park. He simply lifted the back tailgate and Anton routinely slid his board in beside it as they had done almost every afternoon for the past two years.

"Hey, you two boys got a sec?" A voice stopped them before they had time to open the doors of the Kombi and climb in.

"Mal." Johnno looked startled as he spun around to face the park's owner. "Look I'm really sorry about parking on the roadway again. I'm just leaving now so I'll get it out of the way."

"Oh that's alright," he brushed the comment aside. Before staring absently at the angle Johnno had parked the Kombi van on despite numerous warnings that all vehicles were to be parked off the roadway. "I was wondering if you two are able to attend a meeting tomorrow afternoon."

"A meeting huh. What kind of meeting?" Anton asked.

"I can't really say too much at the moment boys," he shrugged the question away while kicking at a loose stone on the roadway. "I was kind of hoping that I could address all the park residents tomorrow. You know, get everyone together."

"All of us?" Anton spoke up, growing concerned that for the first time he could recall, the permanent residents of the holiday park were going to be called together for anything other than a booze up or a barbeque.

"Is everything okay Mal?" Johnno questioned him. "This hasn't got anything to do with rumors of you closing down the recreation room has it? 'Cause we've been trying to keep the noise down when we play pool at night."

"Look, you two boys haven't got anything to worry about," Mal tried desperately to reassure them. "Just be outside the

17

office tomorrow at half past three if you can make it. I really can't say anything until then okay."

"Yeah, we'll be there for sure."

"Okay. See you then," Mal replied with a nod of his head. He was a short, roly-poly sort of man wearing matching khaki shorts and shirt, and a ridiculous comb over on top of his head that saw a few well oiled strands of black hair clinging desperately to his bald scalp.

Anton and Johnno watched as he marched off down the roadway through the center of the park, like a general inspecting his troops prior to sending them off to war. On one side of the roadway were late model RV's and campers belonging to the families that now occupied the grassy field that otherwise sat vacant outside of holiday season. On the other side of the little roadway was a motley crew of aging mobile homes and sagging trailers that had long since plied the highway leading from the city to Kings Beach. That side of the roadway was of course the side that Anton and Johnno lived on, and together the dozen or so permanent residents provided Mal with at least some source of steady income through the quieter months.

"What do you think all that was about?" Johnno asked as he slid into the driver's seat and pulled the seatbelt over his shoulder.

"I don't really know." Anton replied, the statement followed by a reflective whistle. "Could be a number of things really, but I'm not going to worry about tomorrow when today is here to be enjoyed."

"Yeah you're right." Johnno agreed. "Today's been nothing but a headache. Let's just go catch some waves before it's over."

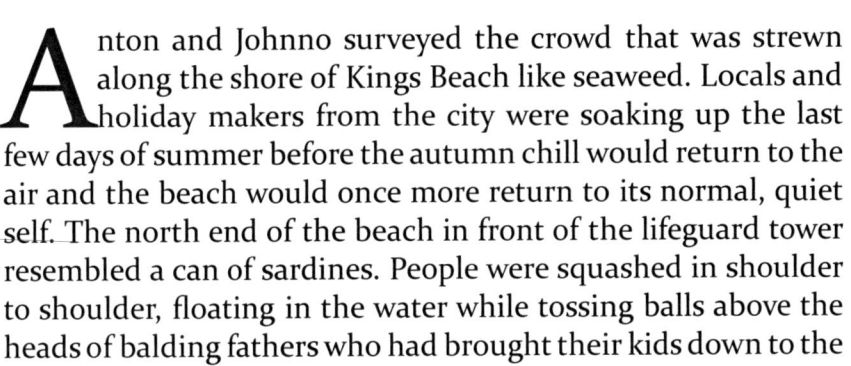

4.20pm

Three is a crowd

nton and Johnno surveyed the crowd that was strewn along the shore of Kings Beach like seaweed. Locals and holiday makers from the city were soaking up the last few days of summer before the autumn chill would return to the air and the beach would once more return to its normal, quiet self. The north end of the beach in front of the lifeguard tower resembled a can of sardines. People were squashed in shoulder to shoulder, floating in the water while tossing balls above the heads of balding fathers who had brought their kids down to the beach at the end of another long hot summer's day. Those same children would squeal with delight when the smallest of waves picked them up on their boogie boards and rushed them head first into a crowd of people standing waist deep in the water.

The scene was repeated at the south end of the beach. Only this time with surfers who sat on their boards with their legs dangling in the water while waiting for anything that resembled a decent wave to appear out of nowhere. When one did there was a mad scramble as up to a dozen surfers paddled frantically for the one wave, only to stand to their feet and watch helplessly as they drifted slowly to a standstill on top of a small, crumbling line of whitewater. It was still over eighty-five degrees and the surf was flat.

"Well, what do you think?" Johnno called dejectedly as he hot-toed across the parking lot in pursuit of Anton.

Ahead of him, Anton had already reached the sanctuary of a small strip of lawn hiding underneath a pandanus tree. Half submerged in a bed of sand that had drifted mercilessly across a concrete path and the small garden bed, it offered the soles of one's feet some respite from the burning surface of the parking lot. Hard enough to find a parking space yet hot enough to fry an egg, it encapsulated everything there was to know about summer in Kings Beach in the few short steps it took to dance from the Kombi to the sand.

"I don't know where you get your surf reports from dude," Anton answered as the rhythmic slapping of leg rope against surfboard caught up to him. "But there's not much happening this afternoon."

"I wish we had some decent swell for a change," Johnno said as he buried the soles of his feet beneath the cool surface of the sand. "We need a hurricane or something off the coast to stir things up a bit before the summer is over."

"Well I don't think that's going to happen."

"Why not?" Johnno asked, surveying the mirror-like surface of the ocean that was offering nothing more than knee high waves in the middle of a heat wave. "We haven't had one this summer."

"Hate to be the one to spoil your party dude, but tomorrow's the last day of summer."

"Oh," Johnno replied flatly.

Anton didn't reply. He just let the word hang there for an eternity. When it came to memories of riding giant waves, tucking into a decent tube ride and feeling the rush of water surge over your head as you drop down the face of a clean late afternoon barrel, this summer had been one of the worst he could remember. Oh pretty much summed it up perfectly!

"Hey boys," a familiar voice called out to them over the

surrounding cries of children and seagulls. "Don't tell me you're seriously thinking of going surfing in that!"

They turned to see their friend Tanya walking towards them.

"Well, we kind of were." Anton laughed as he pointed in the direction of the surfers sitting motionless on their boards behind them. "I think it's the anticipation of a perfect wave that keeps drawing us back like the proverbial moth to the flame."

"Looks more like a bunch of losers lined up for tickets to a concert that is already sold-out if you ask me." Tanya giggled in her usual girly manner. To her there was always something funny to be found in anything.

Tanya Sorenson was a close friend of Anton. She was the waitress at Mermaids, the café that sat perched overlooking the beach on the other side of the parking lot, and saw the boys almost every day. Usually each morning shortly after the café would open. Somewhere between the time the two would return from surfing and the moment Johnno would jump to his feet and say, 'Oh no, I'm going to be late for work again!'

Wearing only a tiny pair of white shorts over a chocolate and gold bikini, Anton thought she resembled a chess piece chiseled by the finger of God himself. In the game of love she was simply check mate, game over. In reality however she was one of the boys. Always there to talk to, share a few jokes with and get dating advice from. Which really sucked! Especially when she had a figure that demanded attention, blonde hair that fell half way down her back and those mysterious brown eyes that had the power to stop a man's heart beating with just one glance in their direction.

Anton had seen it all before. There was always one smooth talking surfer that walked through the door of the café and thought he was in with a chance of landing a date simply because he ordered the breakfast special and asked how she was doing. He'd known Tanya long enough to know that her expectations were high. Way too high for even him to imagine that a girl like her would ever end up with a guy like him. Not only was she a Christian, she was only waitressing she'd remind him at every opportunity until she met Mr Right and sailed off into the sunset for a lifelong cruise and cocktails at six. And by Mr Right she obviously didn't imply him.

"Hi Tanya," Johnno suddenly broke Anton's train of thought. "Not working this afternoon?"

"Of course not," she laughed. "I always finish my shift as soon as the lunch rush is over. The afternoons are mine."

"Yeah it'd be nice to only have to work half the day." Johnno tried his best to keep the conversation moving. Unfortunately it didn't work.

"What time do you start work Johnno?" She asked him sternly, and suddenly her mysterious brown eyes were doing their best to hold back the raging fires of a woman scorned.

"Ah, about half past seven," he mumbled coyly. Once again realizing he had crossed the line and ventured into the conversational abyss from which there was no return, or forgiveness.

"Yeah, well think about that when you stumble out of bed tomorrow morning," she said matter-of-factly. "I'm usually at work before five, getting ready to cook your breakfast and brew your coffee. I'm the one who has to go to bed early each night instead of staying up late and getting drunk."

"I know, I know, I'm sorry," Johnno apologized.

Tanya knew that Johnno was truly sorry. The truth was she just didn't like him. He was too oafish and clumsy with words. Unlike Anton who would unexpectedly come out with the most amazing things. Deep down she knew he always meant well, and he was a good friend to Anton so she had learnt to accept him. She just wished that he'd learn to take the hint that she wasn't at all interested in him. He was always looking for a common interest that wasn't there or a chance to ask her out on a date that was never going to happen. There was however a certain sweetness about him that she found endearing, and she worried that if he sensed that she found him attractive in any way that he would only try even harder to impress her. The thought of which only annoyed her even more.

"That's alright Johnno," she collected her emotions and apologized on a level which surprised even her. "It's just most people don't realize that the afternoon is all I have."

"That's exactly why we are both going to catch a wave and let you enjoy the rest of it." Anton stepped in to smooth over what had become an awkward moment. "So will we be seeing you tomorrow Tanya for another palatable orgy of the taste buds?"

Tanya blushed, smiled and then laughed once more the way she always did when digesting words that came from Anton's mouth.

"Sure," she said. "I was just on my way to the store to get something for Pookie's dinner."

"Ah Pookie, how has the little pooch been lately?" Anton asked her.

"She's been just fine." Tanya's face lit up with the thought of her pet Shi-Tzu. "I was going to bring her for a walk, but it was too hot for the poor little thing. So I left her at home in the air-conditioning."

"You leave the air-conditioning on for your dog?" Johnno sounded bewildered at the thought. "Isn't that kind of expensive?"

"Well how would you like to be locked up in a hot apartment all day in heat like this?" She threw her accusing eyes in Johnno's direction once more. "That's animal abuse."

"I don't know," Johnno answered defensively. "It's just that I can't imagine what it must be like to live in air-conditioning, I work on a hot construction site all day long."

"And I'm pretty much in a mobile home for most of the day," Anton pondered before whistling out loud. "That's one pretty lucky pooch Tanya."

"Well it's nothing but the best for my little Pookie-wookie," she giggled. "We girls need a bit of luxury you know."

"Yeah, well we boys need to immerse our souls in the sweet rapture of the ocean and become one with the water. You know how it is, yin and yang and all the rest."

"I understand Anton," Tanya laughed. "Well don't let me stop you two. Go surf."

"See you for breakfast then." Anton flashed a cheeky grin in her direction and then motioned for Johnno to follow him.

"See you," was all Johnno could manage to say as he stepped off the small strip of grass and immediately remembered just how hot the parking lot was beneath his feet.

The two boys hot-toed it across the remainder of the parking lot and made it to the steps in front of the café that led down to the beach.

Tanya slowly set off in the other direction along the footpath that led away from the café towards her apartment. The air-conditioned apartment halfway up the hill overlooking Kings Beach she shared only with her dog Pookie. Tonight however Pookie would have the whole apartment to herself. She was going out to dinner with none other than Sebastian Wolsey. *The* Sebastian Wolsey, the man who wrote *Road to Nowhere* and that other less memorable book that he no longer liked to talk about but she had enjoyed just the same. It had taken almost a year of persistent pleading from the man before she had finally agreed to go out for dinner with him. Or was it a date? She hoped not. What would her parents have thought about her dating a man who wasn't a Christian? Let alone the idea of going on a date with a man who was twelve years older than her. But it was just dinner she reminded herself, and she had agreed only because he truly was a gentleman, even if he was thirty-eight years old.

She took one last look over her shoulder at the two boys as they made their way down to the beach and immediately caught Johnno's eyes that were already trained firmly in her direction.

Their eyes locked, she smiled uncomfortably for a passing second or two and immediately hated herself for doing so.

Turning away again, she closed her eyes and tried to shake the thought of him from her mind like she had a hundred times before. It didn't work. All she could picture was the sight of his gleaming torso dressed only in a pair of white board shorts with a surfboard under his arm. She closed her eyes again. Tighter this time, only to have her thoughts turn to the surfboard. Picturing its long slender shape pinned under the weight of his firm, buffed body. Not exactly the thoughts that should be going through a Christian girl's mind.

"Yuk!" She said out loud and once more shook the thought of him from her mind. Only this time she walked straight into a woman on rollerblades coming from the other direction.

The impact sent her flying. She landed on her back in a small garden bed beside the footpath, tiny branches scratching against her smooth, tanned skin.

"Hey! Why don't you watch where you're going?" The woman immediately yelled at her.

"Sorry, are you okay?" Tanya asked as she sat up.

"I would be if you weren't walking around with your eyes closed," she growled back. "Try to be more careful."

Tanya ignored the woman as she got to her feet and skated off in her skimpy denim shorts, t-shirt and matching helmet, knee and elbow pads. Instead she was looking in the direction of where she had last seen Anton and Johnno, expecting to see them come running towards her at any moment. Only they were already gone.

"Ouch," she said aloud as she touched a tiny trickle of blood on her back, feeling the tenderness of the scratch on her skin.

In a perfect world a man would have come running to her rescue she thought. Any man except for Johnno. Well maybe if they looked like Johnno it would be alright. Perhaps if she could get Anton's carefree personality in Johnno's body and the gentlemanly qualities of Sebastian thrown in for good measure, then maybe she would have Mr Right. Now there was a thought. Instead she pulled herself to her feet and set off for home, again shaking away any thoughts she had of Johnno's body glistening in the afternoon sun.

7.00pm

Is this a date?

Tanya pursed her lips together and checked that she had applied just the right amount of lip-gloss. Enough that anyone could see her lips matched her red dress perfectly, but not enough that her lips stole all the attention. It was after all only dinner. Although it was also an opportunity to finally wear the little red dress she had seen in a boutique window on Main Street and simply had to have.

She checked her watch. Was he running late or was she running early? She wasn't completely sure, but it did give her time to make a last minute check that everything was in perfect order. Her lipstick looked fine, as did her eye shadow, hair and make-up. She couldn't remember the last time she had gone to so much effort in getting ready to go out and already the evening seemed exciting. Finally she picked up the small bottle of perfume from her dresser drawer and sprayed a mist of it around her neck. It may only have been the same fragrance she wore most days, but in the company of her gold evening purse and new red dress it smelled even more wonderful than she had ever remembered. Her mother would have gushed over how pretty she looked had she had still been alive.

The thought instantly filled her with guilt. What would her mother have thought of her going out for the evening with

Sebastian? She would have thought he was a great writer no doubt, but was he a Christian? The truth was she didn't know. It had never occurred to her to ask him. Surely he knew that she was a Christian. She had used it as an excuse plenty of times when turning down his invitations to join him for dinner in the past. So why had she so suddenly agreed to accompany him tonight? Maybe it was just Sebastian's gentle persistence, or the fact that she finally wanted to go out for the evening somewhere nicer than the pizza parlor. Or perhaps it was just an excuse to finally wear the little red dress she had bought. Either way it was just dinner.

Then why was she feeling so excited at the thought of going out for the evening with this man?

She honestly didn't know. She couldn't sit still. Her heart was racing a million miles an hour and she had never recalled fussing this much over the way she looked at all before in her life. Anyone would tell her that it was nothing more than a case of nervousness before stepping out on a date. But it wasn't a date, it was just dinner.

Who cares anyway? Sebastian was a gentleman and it was about time someone in her life stepped up to the plate and showed her how a lady should be treated. If she had left it to Anton and Johnno to plan the evening, she'd probably be sitting in a folding chair by now dressed in shorts and t-shirt, eating chicken from a bucket and watching helplessly as they plied Sebastian with one beer after another. Even if it was a date, what was the harm in simply going out to dinner? If ever she was to have a chance of finding Mr Right she at least had to know what to expect when it came to going out for the evening.

The knock on the front door sounded loudly, shaking her from her thoughts. With her heart beating wildly she checked her lip-gloss and hair one more time in the mirror and hurried to the front door.

"Tanya, you look breathtaking." Sebastian greeted her the

moment she threw the door open. "For a moment I thought I had the wrong apartment."

Tanya had no idea what he meant. She had written down the same number for him on a piece of paper that clearly matched the one on her door. But it made her feel weak at the knees and giggle just the same.

"Sebastian, you're right on time," she said without even looking down at her watch.

"Are you ready to go?" He asked her, still taking in the sight of her in the red dress.

"Yeah, of course," she smiled.

"Then great, let's head off. I've know this great little Italian restaurant I'm sure you're going to love."

"Can I ask a question before we go?" She suddenly blurted out, surprising even herself that the question escaped her lips.

"Sure, what is it?"

"Is this a date?" She looked up at him with an innocent yet confused expression plastered across her face.

Sebastian smiled warmly while he took a moment to think of the right answer.

"Let's not start the evening with that sort of pressure shall we?" He reassured her. "I've really been looking forward to this for so long. I have a table reserved for us and I'm sure we'll think of what we can call the evening over dinner. Besides, aren't you a little hungry by now?"

"Hungry like you could not imagine." Tanya smiled as she stepped out of her apartment.

Sebastian had no idea what she meant, but he liked the sound of it just the same.

8.30pm

Late night chicken dinners

"You want some more chicken?" Anton asked as he got up from the folding chair, still licking his fingers from the last piece he had stripped down to the bone.

"No mate. I'm stuffed," Johnno groaned as he slouched back in the chair outside Anton's trailer home and gazed up at the stars overhead.

"Same with me," Anton agreed. "Maybe we shouldn't have bought two barbeque chickens."

"Not to mention the fries."

"Yeah, that too."

"Want me to take care of the dishes?"

"No. I've got it covered dude," Anton said as he took the empty paper plate from him, grabbed his own and walked a grand total of fourteen steps to the trash can where he dutifully lifted the lid and tossed them in. "Dishes are done man!"

Anton stretched his arms above his head as he slowly shuffled his way back towards where they had set up the folding chairs and table on the grassy lawn outside his trailer. Once again it had proved too hot to eat inside, and when the stars were this bright why wouldn't anyone want to sit outside? It was moments like these that he had learnt to appreciate. The simple ones, where eating dinner outside on a starry summer's night made it feel like you were on holidays.

The truth was that Anton had been on holidays since the day he dropped out of high school. Simply deciding one day that enough was enough and walking out of the classroom halfway through an English class after disagreeing with the teacher over having to base his end of year assignment on a selected play by William Shakespeare. Forget Shakespeare, the man was dead and had long been overrated. Okay, maybe that was being a little harsh. After all, when you're talking about perhaps the greatest playwright of all time the name deserves all the respect it has earned over the centuries.

'Well excuse me for begging to differ,' he recalled saying as he stood to his feet in the middle of a packed classroom. He could still picture the stunned expression on Suzie Mears' face as she turned around in the front row. Eyes as wide open as her mouth, two rows of silver braces protruding from her cute, cherry red lips that he still regretted never getting the chance to kiss. 'But perhaps I'm ready to make the decision for myself on what constitutes a great poet. There are plenty of talented, modern poets out there who are struggling for just a sliver of our attention. Seems to me though that all the government is keen to do in the public school system is ram some long dead, has been down our throats because it suits their political agenda.'

In that moment Anton recalled, he became both a spokesman for poets everywhere and a political activist. Surely that had to leave a lasting impression on the mind of little Suzie Mears, teacher's pet who always sat in the front row. Later he had moved out of home with some older friends and later still had hit the road, left the city behind and headed to Kings Beach. That was six years ago.

It only occurred to him in the years that followed that William Shakespeare really had nothing at all to do with his rebelliousness at the time. It had stemmed from being turned

31

down by Suzie Mears when he had asked her to the school dance. One moment of madness had seemingly defined his life and it had all been over a girl. In fact Anton had later made a point to borrow some of Shakespeare's more notable works from the local library, Hamlet, Macbeth, A Midsummer Night's Dream and of course Romeo and Juliet. Although it wasn't enough to make him a huge fan of his writing, he realized now that if he'd played by the rules back in high school that he'd probably have topped his English class. Who knows? Perhaps he would have finished high school and ended up somewhere else rather than in a trailer park, scraping chicken bones into a trash can and wondering if little Suzie Mears ever read the one poem he had published in some obscure magazine that went bust.

"No, don't buy into it," he said aloud. "If you believe that you'll believe every other bogus idea."

"What was that?" Johnno looked up at him strangely.

"Oh, nothing." Anton stopped dead in his tracks, suddenly feeling embarrassed.

"Are you talking to yourself again Anton? 'Cause you know that's not a good thing right?"

"Leave me alone," he light-heartedly brushed his comment aside. "I was just thinking out loud, that's all."

"Yeah, well no more beer for you."

"What are you crazy?"

"Hey, I'm not the one who's walking around talking to myself."

"Okay, okay. So I was talking to myself again, so what!" Anton said slowly. "It's not a problem."

"Are you sure?" Johnno asked as he eased back into his chair. "'Cause that's the fourth time this week I've caught you doing that, and it's only Tuesday."

"Are you counting me?" Anton seemed taken aback. "That's cold dude."

Johnno ignored him.

"You can't just walk around talking to yourself and expect people to not think that you're a little crazy. Are you sure you're feeling fine?"

"Yes I'm sure," Anton sighed. "It was just something I had on my mind, there now it's gone."

"Yeah, well sometimes I wish I knew what goes on inside that head of yours."

"Nothing goes on inside my head okay," Anton protested. "Thanks to your twenty questions I don't even remember what I was thinking about now, are you happy?"

"Alright. Just don't do it again."

Anton sighed as he sat down in the chair beside him. He ran his fingers through his scruffy dark blonde hair and looked up at the stars above. There wasn't a cloud in the sky yet the humidity clung to his body like a wet shirt.

"Whoa, who needs TV when you've got stars like this?" Anton finally broke the silence.

"I'm sorry, you talking to me or your invisible little friend?" Johnno teased him.

"Okay, knock it off." Anton laughed, knowing full well that he wasn't going to let it go so easily.

"I can't see anyone else here," Johnno joked as he got to his feet, pretending to look around for somebody before calling loudly. "Hey Anton's friend, where are you?"

"Okay, you've had your fun," Anton laughed. "Now sit down before Mal races over here all worked up and tells us to keep the noise down."

"Mate, you're absolutely right." Johnno composed himself before comically attempting to sit down and following up with a fart loud enough to be heard throughout the trailer park. "Oh no! I think I just sat on him!"

"That's rotten dude!" Anton erupted into a fit of laughter.

"Hey I found your friend Anton," Johnno burst out laughing.

"Anything you want to say to him now? Because I think he's dying."

"Smells like you're dying."

"Alright boys," a voice quietly interrupted them from their impromptu comedy routine. "It's going on nine o'clock so can we keep the noise down to a minimum please?"

Anton and Johnno looked up to see Mal standing in the middle of the roadway with a flashlight in hand, shining it in their direction. He'd obviously been in the process of making his final rounds for the night when he'd been drawn to Anton's trailer site by the growing noise.

"Sorry Mal, it won't happen again," Anton apologized.

"Very well, I won't need to come back here later then will I?" He asked firmly.

"Not at all Mal. You have a good night then," Johnno said.

Mal didn't say anything further. He just waved his hand in acknowledgement and strode off in the other direction. Johnno quietly watched him leave until finally he had disappeared from view.

"Hey, what do you think is up with Mal?" He finally asked Anton.

"I don't know dude. Maybe it's got something to do with that smell you let go before," Anton smiled, at the same time trying not to get Johnno worked up again. "Probably because it's nearly nine, you know the park's minimum noise policies as well as I do."

"No, not that," Johnno said seriously. "Ever since this afternoon when he mentioned that meeting tomorrow, he sort of hasn't been himself. I wish I knew what was going on."

"Who knows dude." Anton settled back quietly in the chair once more and gazed up at the stars. "He did say we didn't have anything to worry about. So my advice is don't worry about it."

"Yeah, I suppose you're right."

"Of course I am," Anton tried to reassure him. "You need to

learn to relax. All you ever do is work, and worry over every little thing that doesn't seem right."

"That's not true."

"Of course it is." Anton turned to look directly at him. "You're always wishing this didn't happen or wishing that was different."

"So what?" Johnno huffed. "What's such a big deal about that?"

"You're wishing your life away dude!" Anton's voice lit up with excitement. "You're putting your life on hold and spending all your time worrying about the future instead of living each day as it comes. Trust me, when the future finally arrives all you're going to do is worry about where all the time went or wish that life could have somehow magically turned out to be different along the way. Let me tell you something, magic doesn't just happen my friend, you have to make it happen!"

"Are you finished?"

"Yes I am," Anton said proudly.

"Good, 'cause after listening to that I'm going to get another beer."

Johnno stood to his feet and walked over towards Anton's trailer, disappearing momentarily beneath the canvas flap of the annex and emerging proudly clutching two bottles of beer. He dropped one into Anton's lap as he passed by his chair, knowing all too well that he'd never catch the bottle if he attempted to throw it, and returned to his slumped position in the folding chair.

"Did you even listen to a word I said?" Anton asked, slightly annoyed that once again his friend had failed to take him seriously.

"Yep," Johnno replied as he twisted the cap off the beer bottle. "There were a lot of words, and something about the future being full of magic wishes."

"It's a crime dude," Anton sighed as he opened the cap and took a swig from the bottle. "Wishing your life away, it's a crime of self."

"Well I wish you'd lighten up a bit," Johnno laughed. "Are you forgetting that we're both living the life we want, just in different ways? I mean surfing in the morning, surfing again in the afternoon and drinking beer under the stars 'till late at night doesn't sound like wishing your life away to me."

"Yeah, maybe you're right," Anton agreed. But Johnno kept talking just the same.

"Sounds like you're the one who could do with a genie in a bottle. What would you wish for? A million bucks, your own private jet and a mansion full of America's top models?"

Anton looked at him carefully before answering.

"The perfect wave."

"Come on, are you serious?" Johnno looked at him in amazement. "If you had a million bucks and your own private jet you could spend your life traveling the world, looking for the perfect wave and all the pretty girls would come along for the ride."

"You're missing the point dude," Anton said calmly. "It's like how they say that surfing isn't just something that you do. It's a way of life. Well a wave is just a wall of water, unless you understand where you belong in the grand scheme of things you'll never be able to figure out how to ride it to shore."

"I still don't understand your point," Johnno admitted once he had tossed the words around carefully in his head.

"It's simple," Anton replied. "There are just some things that money can't buy. Money is purely a means to exist, and I exist just fine without any."

Last Day of Summer

5.10am

Another early morning sunrise

A nton reached over and belted the alarm clock, effectively cutting short the weatherman's report that today was going to be another scorcher. Who needed a man on the radio to tell them that anyway? He'd had enough trouble getting a solid nights' sleep from tossing and turning all night long in the stifling humidity that had left the bed sheets drenched and the mobile home resembling something more like a toaster oven.

He swung his feet over the side of the bed, immediately feeling the grit on the floor of the trailer from a week's supply of sand he had walked inside. Maybe today he should make sure he gave it a sweep out. Well, maybe he'd at least think about it. Pausing to grab a carton of orange juice from the door of the small refrigerator, he walked over to where his board shorts lay waiting, draped over the end of the kitchen table.

"It's going to be some kind of day," he whispered out loud while peering through the window of the trailer. He watched quietly as the sky grew into a brilliant shade of morning blue while sipping the juice straight from the carton.

"Whoa dude. Put some pants on for crying out loud!" The voice made Anton spin around in a hurry.

"No, no, no. Don't turn around," Johnno lamely protested as he quickly shielded his eyes from the sight of Anton standing naked in the doorway of the trailer. "I wish I didn't have to see that!"

"You're early."

"You're naked," Johnno protested as he continued to hold a hand over his eyes. "Well don't just stand there. Hurry up and put something on."

"Oh right. Sorry dude." Anton quickly grabbed his faded red board shorts from the kitchen table and slipped them on. "Did the heat wake you up early too?"

"Wake me up?" Johnno groaned. "I could hardly get to sleep at all. I've been up since half past four."

"Why didn't you come over and get me then? We could have just gone down to the beach a little earlier."

"Because I was afraid I'd see you walking around like I did just then." Johnno stepped into the van, satisfied now that his friend finally had some pants on. "Honestly mate, who stands around naked drinking juice from a carton anyway?"

"It's just a natural thing dude." Anton brushed the whole episode aside and held out the juice carton in front of him. "Want some? It's orange and mango."

"Yeah sure," Johnno said as he took the carton from him. He proceeded to guzzle its contents before handing it back to Anton.

Anton finished what little juice remained and placed the empty carton on the kitchen table.

"You ready to go then?" Anton asked as he grabbed his wallet and house key from where he kept them in the cupboard above the cook top and made his way to the door.

"I'm ready when you are," Johnno said as he stepped out into the annex.

"Oh, I almost forgot Tanya's birthday gift," Anton said as he hurried back inside once more.

"But her birthday party isn't until tonight," Johnno sighed. "Can't you get it later? We're wasting time."

"But I wanted to give it to her this morning," he replied

quickly. "Besides, I have to grab a few other things for today anyway. It will only take a second."

Johnno simply shook his head and stepped outside to wait impatiently.

Inside Anton quickly packed a towel, some deodorant, and a change of clothes into a small backpack, being careful to place the small gift wrapped package on top before zipping the bag shut. After locking the trailer door he slipped his flip-flops onto his feet, grabbed his surfboard that was leaning quietly in the corner of the annex and followed Johnno outside.

Johnno already had his surfboard and towel packed in the back of the Kombi van. Anton simply slid his board in through the open tailgate like he did every morning and climbed into the front passenger seat. The motor turned over and the Kombi spluttered to life. Slowly Johnno weaved the van through the maze of parked vehicles and onto the narrow asphalt roadway that sliced its way down the middle of the trailer park.

As they neared the entrance, they caught sight of Mal as he stepped outside of the house at the front of the holiday park that also doubled as the reception office. He waved to them as they drove past, just as he did every morning at around half past five. No doubt off to begin his daily chores of checking on the park, cleaning the barbeques, restocking the amenities block and everything else he usually did to keep the park looking clean and presentable.

"Do you think he looks a bit...? I don't know, droopy this morning?" Johnno asked as the Kombi pulled out onto the road for the short drive to the beach."

"Droopy? Is that even a word?" Anton laughed as the van roared its way up through the gears.

"Yeah. Of course it is," Johnno said defensively. "You know, sad, glum, a bit down in the dumps."

"I didn't notice to tell the truth," Anton admitted. "Did you think he looked a bit depressed?"

"I thought so, but maybe I'm wrong. I mean why should today be any different for him, right?"

"Well it is the last day of summer," Anton offered. "Maybe he's just sad that the tourist season will soon be over."

"Are you kidding?" Johnno retorted. "Come winter and the park is full of gray nomads. If you ask me it's almost like a convoy of retirees passing through town. No, I think more likely it's the meeting that he wants everyone at this afternoon. I wish I knew what it was all about."

"Would you let it go dude?" Anton mocked him. "Nothing is going to happen okay, it's probably just to organize another barbeque before your so-called 'gray nomads' all arrive."

"Still I won't be able to make it. I don't finish work until half past three and that's the same time he wants to have this meeting."

"So, just get there when you get there," Anton brushed his comment aside. "You know Mal, it's no big deal. Nothing is ever a big deal. We'll probably be just getting started on the beer by the time you rock up."

"Yeah, you're right." Johnno let the conversation fall into silence.

Outside the morning was only beginning to come alive. Walkers were out enjoying the early morning sunlight as it glistened on the calm surface of the river that the road followed the short distance to the beach. The holiday park was in the perfect location Anton thought as they drove along. Nestled right along the riverfront near the mouth of the river and set only a couple of blocks back from the main shopping strip, it was within walking distance of Kings Beach. Although most of the time the thought of scaling the steep hills to get to the surf beach saw the boys continually buckle up in the Kombi to drive the short distance.

On cue, the road twisted and climbed as it neared the mouth of the river, and the Kombi groaned as Johnno worked it back

41

through the gears. Fourth, third and then back down to second before beginning the easy descent to the parking lot between the surf club and the café where Tanya worked. The Volkswagen, Anton thought must surely be capable of following the route on autopilot by now. It barely traveled outside of the triangle defined by the trailer park, the beach and the construction site where Johnno worked.

Johnno glided the van into the usual parking space outside Mermaids Café like he did every morning and the two hopped out excitedly. The sight of long clean lines greeted them for as far as the eye could see. The sun had already climbed well above the horizon, and right now the surface of the ocean glistened with a thousand diamonds dancing across the waves as they rolled into shore. It was like finding a lost treasure at the end of an epic movie. In a summer that had continually delivered only waist high waves at best, summer had decided to go out with a bang. Surfers dropped down into clean six foot waves and tucked in for a pipe ride as the waves curled and broke overhead. Neither could remember the last time they had seen a morning quite like this.

"Come on Johnno," Anton beckoned to his friend to hurry up and lock the van. "It's the last day of summer and the Sea Gods have dished us up a peace offering."

"Alright mate," Johnno replied as he teasingly applied some more wax to his surfboard.

"Can you do that any slower?" Anton nearly shouted at him.

"Nope." Johnno laughed. "You might want some though. The last thing you want to do when we've finally got some decent swell is slip just when you're about to tuck into a nice barrel."

"Yeah okay," Anton agreed reluctantly.

Johnno threw the wax to his friend and watched in amusement as Anton juggled the lump of surfboard wax three times before catching it. He then proceeded to apply it so vigorously that he was worried his friend might tear a muscle in his arm or dislocate his shoulder. Finally Anton stopped and tossed the wax straight past him to where it landed safely in the back of the Kombi.

"Well what are you waiting for?" Anton asked from underneath his tangle of dark blonde hair. "Let's go."

Johnno just smiled. Though Anton may be the kind of person to get passionate about the most bizarre things in life, when he became excited it was a little scary.

"Yeah alright mate. Keep your pants on!" Johnno laughed.

With nothing else to say, the two ran excitedly across the parking lot and onto the cool sand.

5.30am

Diary of Painted Toenails

Tanya stood at the edge of the water and watched as the remainder of another perfect wave finally reached the shore and rushed over her freshly painted toenails. She may have been dressed only in her usual attire of black shorts and matching black t-shirt with the motif of a mermaid, ready to start another day of work at the café, but at least her toenails looked pretty.

Not just pretty, but dazzling she thought as the water rushed back out to sea between her feet. She'd stayed up late last night, sitting on the end of her bed with her pet dog Pookie and painting her nails to resemble the sea. Not the sandy green color of the ocean in front of her. More like the shimmery, turquoise color she remembered from when she had last holidayed on an island in The Great Barrier Reef, alone.

Last night had been a disaster. How long was she destined to go through life like this? When it came to men, she realized her life was a tangled mess of insecurity and high expectations. Her evening with Sebastian had only highlighted the problem. Poor Sebastian. The thought had kept her up late into the evening with only Pookie to keep her company. As much as she loved her dog, a part of her was crying out for more. She wanted to love and feel love in return. She wanted the rush of a first kiss, to feel the tingle it sent down her spine all the way to her toes. She wanted to be immersed in the feeling. To feel it encompass her whole body and rush over her skin like the waves rushing over her feet. Most of all, she wanted to not feel alone. She wanted a man. Last night she finally had a chance to fulfill her desires. Only she choked, and in the process had probably inflicted some kind of deep emotional damage on the man that would take some time to heal.

Tanya felt torn between asking God for His direction in the matter, and allowing her mind to wonder what it might have felt like to find herself wrapped in the arms of a man this morning. Curled up together in her bed between the crisp, cotton bed sheets, and watching the morning sunlight stream in through the window instead of standing alone on the shore. Was there really such a thing as the perfect man? Or should she have settled for second best? Right now she wished she hadn't said such a thing to Sebastian last night after he had walked her home from the restaurant. She had invited him inside for coffee, not realizing that coffee to him had meant something more. However that first rushed kiss, hot and intense while pressed against the wall had cleared her mind of any misunderstanding. So she had slapped him and made it clear, in no uncertain terms, that she wasn't about to give up her Christian morals for someone who clearly wasn't the right person to spend the rest of her life with. Finally after some earnest apologizing for his manners he had left. Walking off into the night and leaving her alone again in her apartment to rue what might have been.

Most nights Tanya wrote in her diary before going to bed. A diary she had kept since her Aunty Dorothy had given it to her on her thirteenth birthday. It was a huge diary of at least five hundred pages, with decorative borders and a cover adorned with fake diamonds and cardboard cut-outs of frangipani flowers. Last night however she had curiously opened it to the first page, and began reading some of the more interesting entries as she flicked through its pages.

The diary started out purely simple. There was a list of things she had received for her birthday. On the next page was a colorful drawing of her Aunty, Mom and Dad. Then followed the usual gossip from school that any Eighth Grade girl thinks is important enough to write down. As she'd flicked further through the diary however, she noticed that it soon became a road map to a young girl's life. Boyfriends came and went, sometimes in the cruelest manner possible. Then somehow life became surprisingly complicated. Even for a young girl going on fifteen. First her cat Tinkerbell died, which was at the time totally devastating. Then news came that Aunty Dorothy had cancer. Just before her sixteenth birthday.

Instead of being a sad time, that summer had turned out to be one of the best summers of her life. Her Mom and Dad had invited her Aunt to join them on holidays at Kings Beach in an apartment overlooking the sea. She got to spend the entire two weeks with her Aunt, building sandcastles, shopping, going out for ice-cream and frolicking about in the water. At nights they would write entries together in her diary about what they did that day, and make a list of things that Tanya promised to do when she grew up. All the while knowing that her Aunt wouldn't be around to see Tanya on the day she got married.

'Always promise me one thing Tanya,' her Aunt had told her while they had walked along the beach one afternoon. 'When you're old enough to start wearing nail polish, make sure you write down not only the name of each color you wear but also why you chose to wear it and what it reminds you of. When you finally write about a color that reminds you of a boy, you'll know you've found the right person to spend the rest of your life with.'

So far no color had ever reminded her of a boy at all.

Her Aunt was there for her sixteenth birthday. A birthday they had celebrated right here on the beach on the last day of their summer holiday. Her father had set sixteen candles on top of a sandcastle as the sun slowly set in the afternoon sky and told her to make a wish. The wishes she made that afternoon were enough to fill her diary. Later that night her Aunt had given Tanya her birthday present. Sixteen bottles of nail polish, all in different shades, and the two had sat up late talking girl talk while she showed Tanya how to do her nails. From that day on her diary had become a diary of painted toenails. A color chart of emotions, dreams and places she'd been whenever she had painted her toenails and stepped out. She would apply a small dab of nail color on the page of her diary, and below it add a few thoughts on how she was feeling. Or make a wish, and in a unique way keep the memory of her Aunt alive.

The diary had helped her through some dark times. Like two weeks after they'd returned to the city from summer holidays with her Aunt. They knew she was sick, but nobody expected her to pass away so soon. The doctors had said it was probably her body's way of knowing that her time was near that allowed her to enjoy the two weeks by the sea before it began to shut down. Her Aunt's funeral was one of only two times that Tanya had ever worn black nail polish, and the entry stood out like a black stain on the page. The other was three years ago, at her parents' funeral.

It was something that no-one ever wants to experience. The chilling phone call telling you that a loved one has been involved in an auto accident and had been rushed to hospital. Tanya still remembered driving back to the city with arms trembling, praying that it was all a mistake. Surely it had to be someone else's parents and not hers. When she arrived at the emergency room however, the horrible reality of the situation was waiting for her. Only she was too late. Just as her Aunt had left this life, so too had they. She was all alone.

They had left the city early that morning, excited to be driving to the coast to see their daughter and only child.

Somewhere on the outskirts of that forsaken city, a trucker had run a red light in a semi-trailer and slammed into the side of her father's car. Killing him instantly and pinning her mother inside the twisted wreckage. She later died at the hospital. It was supposed to be a happy day. They were going to stay over for the night, eat take-out on the beach at sunset and build a sandcastle with twenty-three candles on it. It was her birthday, just as it was today and she never got the chance to make a wish.

Tanya blinked back the tears. Her eyes strained to admire the tiny diamonds dancing across the surface of the waves in the brilliant morning sunshine. It was hard to believe that another year had passed, and here she was now twenty six years old and still to figure out the secret to life. Life was more than a puppy waiting to lick your toes when you came home from your job every afternoon. It was more than making the perfect cup of coffee in a café overlooking the sea. And it was certainly more than writing silly entries in a diary each night and feeling so alone while you painted your toenails. At least that was the decision she had reached last night as she lay on her bed listening to the sound of the waves crashing on the shore. By the time she finally drifted off to sleep, she had thought of the perfect way to celebrate her birthday. The thought made her smile.

Tanya glanced quickly at her watch, suddenly surprised at what time it was. Knowing that she should soon be starting work, she turned from the scene and began to run back up the beach towards the café.

6.30am

Genie in a Bottle

"Let's go and get something to eat. I'm getting hungry dude," Anton called as he paddled over to where Johnno sat on his board with his legs dangling in the water.

"One more wave," Johnno replied with eyes focused on the horizon. The next line of swell was building steadily as it rolled towards shore.

"Don't you have to go to work today?" Anton asked.

"Thanks for reminding me," Johnno replied sarcastically. "You think I didn't know that already?"

"I was more worried you'd forgotten about getting something to eat. Seriously, I'm starving here dude!"

Johnno heard him, but his concentration had switched to the clean blue line of water that was rolling towards him.

"Meet you on shore then," Johnno called over his shoulder as he turned and paddled frantically. Behind him a wave had built to the point of forming a perfect crest, waiting for him to glide down the face of its smooth, mirror-like surface.

Anton watched as the wave picked his friend up. Johnno stood to his feet before momentarily disappearing on the other side of a six foot wall of water. A second later he appeared again, surfboard whacking the crest of the wave as he pulled off a maneuver that sent water spraying in his wake. And then he was gone again. Anton watched as the wave collapsed behind him. A turbulent, thundering crash that was powerful enough to suck the sand from the ocean floor. The wave churned into a streaky mix of sandy green and white before Johnno appeared once more, still standing as he rode the wall of whitewater into shore.

Anton smiled for a moment before he lined up the next wave, then paddled as fast as he could towards the shore. He felt the surge as the wave caught him. It lifted him up and began to rush him forward. Standing to his feet, Anton felt the adrenalin pump through his body as he raced down the wave and turned sharply at the bottom, ready to copy Johnno's move he had seen only moments earlier. Somehow it went terribly wrong. He felt the surfboard wobble beneath his feet, followed quickly by the sensation of being turned upside down as the wave picked him up and threw him forward. Then the board disappeared from beneath his feet and Anton went over the falls. Free falling into nothing before finally hitting the shallow water in front of the wave.

At first there was nothing, and then the wave crashed down on him, surfboard and all. Feeling himself tumbling over and over, Anton did his best to hold his breath while he was underwater. Finally he came to the surface, coughing for air and struggling to get to his feet. Johnno was already sloshing through the water to reach him. Luckily the leg rope was still attached to his surfboard. So Anton simply pulled it towards him and tucked it under his arm as he stood up.

"Man, are you alright?" He asked as Anton struggled to catch his breath. "It looked like you took a pretty hard fall."

"Yeah I'm fine," Anton lied as he made his way out of the water.

"What happened?"

"I don't know dude. I just got dumped, that's all."

"Are you going to be okay?"

"Yeah. Just as soon as you stop asking me questions and I get something to eat." Anton playfully punched him on the shoulder.

"Come on. Let's go see what Tanya is up to," Johnno laughed.

"I'm right behind you," Anton said as he sloshed knee-high through the water before tripping on something that was hidden beneath the surface and falling once more. "Oh man! What did I just stub my toe on?"

Johnno turned to see his friend sitting in the water and holding his big toe with a look of pain on his face.

"What did you do?"

"I stubbed my toe on this," Anton said as he held up an old piece of driftwood that once may have resembled a part of a tree branch. "It was on the bottom of the sand. I guess it must have washed into shore with the morning tide, or the swell. It's been a while since the ocean has been stirred up like this."

"You can't say you're okay this time," Johnno said as he looked closely at his foot. "Your toe's bleeding man."

"I'll be fine dude. It's just a scrape," Anton said as he stood up once more and washed his foot in the water. "Come on. Let's go eat."

"Yeah you're right about the ocean being churned up," Johnno said as he reached down and caught a glass bottle as it bobbed up and down on the remnants of the next wave. "The swell is washing everything into shore this morning."

"Don't you just hate litterbugs?" Anton snarled as he looked at the bottle in Johnno's hand. "I wish they'd put their rubbish in the bin instead of throwing it into the ocean."

"Hey I think there's a message inside." Johnno proudly held the glass bottle up for his friend to see.

Anton walked over to where his friend held the green wine bottle. Sure enough it contained a rolled up note inside. Johnno was shaking it, trying to figure out how he was going to get it out.

"You're going to need a corkscrew to open it dude," Anton laughed.

"I wonder where it has come from. For all we know this could have floated around the world for a hundred years or more. Maybe there's a genie inside." Johnno seemed curious as he tried to rub the bottle.

"There's no way there is a genie inside," Anton mocked him.

"How do you know?" Johnno looked at him sternly. "Maybe I'm just not rubbing the bottle the right way."

"Because you rub a lamp to summon a genie," Anton laughed. "Give me a look at it."

"Wasn't there a song about a genie in a bottle or something like that?" Johnno asked as he passed him the bottle.

"It's not a genie okay. Besides, that song was about a girl."

"How do you know?"

"Are we talking about the song now or the bottle?"

"The bottle," he laughed.

"Because judging by the label it was once a bottle of Shiraz Cabernet. No more than two years old. Probably cost around eight dollars on sale at your local bottle mart," Anton remarked proudly.

"So it's just a message in a bottle then?"

"That's right," Anton said. "Still I wonder what it says."

"Or how long it's been floating around in the ocean," Johnno added.

"I'd say not long," Anton sighed in disbelief at his friend's inability to recognize the clues.

"How can you be so sure?" Johnno asked as he huddled in closer to get a better look.

"Because the label is still attached," he said as he pointed to the bright red label with the gold letters stamped on it. "Surely a label like this couldn't survive in the ocean any more than a day or so."

"So when do you think whoever wrote the message tossed it into the sea?" Johnno asked. His curiosity was now fully aroused.

"I'd guess either last night or early this morning."

"So what are we going to do with it?" Johnno looked at him for an answer.

"First we're going to go and get breakfast," Anton smiled. "Then we're going to open it."

6.50am

Pleased to meet you

"Hi boys. How was the surf this morning?" Tanya asked as she walked up to the same outside table that Anton and Johnno occupied almost every morning.

"Totally sick," Johnno exclaimed. Once again he tried to impress Tanya in the hope of coming across cool. As usual he failed, miserably.

"Yeah. You don't look too well," Tanya teased him by acting like she didn't understand what he implied.

"No I meant it was awesome," Johnno tried again. "You know, really good."

"Now you feel good?" Tanya looked at him stupidly. "Make up your mind Johnno. Do you feel sick or good?"

"No, I mean it was... nice." He said sheepishly.

"Ah, nice," she continued to play him along. "Is that a word all you surfies are using now?"

"Ah never mind," he sighed as he slumped back in his chair.

"So what's it going to be this morning?" She turned to ask Anton, totally ignoring Johnno for the moment.

"I'll have a cappuccino and the sausage and scrambled eggs on toast Tan," Anton said without needing to check the menu. "And you can have a happy birthday."

"Oh, you remembered," she smiled sweetly in return.

Tanya liked the way Anton would simply call her Tan from time to time. It made her feel like one of the gang. To her it was a reassuring way of knowing that they were comfortable with just being friends. She knew that there was no way she could ever be interested in someone like Anton. It would just be gross. Not in a repulsive way. More like the thought of dating your cousin. There was some kind of defense mechanism inside that stopped your thoughts from even wanting to go there.

"Yeah I almost forgot. Happy birthday Tanya," Johnno spoke up after it appeared she had forgotten to take his order. "Can I order a cappuccino and two slices of raisin toast please?"

Without saying anything she looked across at the buff surfer slouched in one of the café chairs, and instinctively her eyes fell to his washboard stomach. Before her thoughts wandered anymore she deliberately turned her eyes to the ocean in front of the café, choosing instead to focus on nothing in particular.

"Okay, I'll be back shortly with the two coffees," she said without needing to write the order down. "It's quiet at the moment so I shouldn't be too long with your order."

"Oh, and can we borrow a corkscrew if it isn't too much trouble?" Johnno asked just as she was about to turn and leave.

"It's a bit early in the morning to be drinking isn't it Johnno?" She turned to look at him, instantly hating the fact that her eyes kept returning to the sight of his half naked torso.

"No, it's just that... Oh never mind," he slouched back in the chair again.

"No it's alright," she suddenly changed her tone of voice. "I'll get one of the other waitresses to bring one over."

Without trying to break eye contact with Johnno, Tanya smiled uneasily at him for a moment. Then she quickly made her way to the kitchen before her thoughts turned to his washboard stomach again. What was wrong with her? Had her date with Sebastian last night finally woken some long forgotten desire to be intimate with a man?

"What is it with that girl?" Johnno whispered as soon as she had left the table. "Do I sound stupid to you? Or does she always seem to have a hard time understanding everything I say?"

"I think she's just having some fun with you dude," Anton smirked. "Don't take it so personal."

"Well I wish she wouldn't. I always end up feeling like an idiot when I'm around her."

"Maybe she likes you," Anton joked with him.

"Don't tease me Anton. You know that I like her," Johnno sighed. "She's got that pretty waitress thing going on. You know what I'm talking about? Not that skinny bikini model look that every girl on the beach is trying to copy. But that curvy, confident, totally feminine look that says this is me and I don't care if I'm slightly curvier than the next girl."

"Have you ever told her about how you feel dude?"

"Are you kidding me? I can't even order breakfast without her shooting me down!" Johnno shook his head at the thought. "But even that isn't enough to stop me liking her."

"Yeah I can see what you mean," Anton tried to hide his own thoughts of Tanya. "She's very pretty dude!"

Anton waited until Tanya had left their sight before he brought the bottle out from under his chair and placed it in the middle of the table.

"Hey, I never noticed these markings before," he said as he turned the bottle over in his hands and examined the row of colored blotches that adorned the base.

"They look like they've been painted on," Johnno remarked as he took a closer look.

Anton ran his fingers over the uneven surface, tracing the colored dots as they formed a complete circle around the base of the bottle. They were all uniform in shape and evenly spaced in varying shades of red, violet and turquoise.

"It looks like someone's painted the dots with nail polish," Anton said as he studied it closely.

"Yeah you're right," Johnno agreed as he took the bottle out of Anton's hands. "I think you'll find our message inside is most likely from a girl."

"There's only one way to find out," Anton said. "We've got to open this thing. Now what's taking so long with that corkscrew?"

The two sat impatiently waiting for a waitress to appear with the corkscrew as Tanya had said. Finally one of the other girls stepped out from inside the café carrying a tray with two cups of coffee balanced on top. She carefully made her way across the timber decked floor and placed the tray down on the table where Anton and Johnno sat overlooking the beach.

"Did one of you ask for a corkscrew?" The waitress asked. She was a dark haired girl of slightly Asian appearance, perhaps in her late twenties. She stood with the corkscrew in her hand waiting for an answer, obviously amused at the thought of someone asking for a corkscrew at seven in the morning.

"We sure did," Johnno spoke up. "We found this bottle washed up on the shore this morning. There's a message inside and we need to pull the cork out to read it."

"Oh, how sweet!" The waitress suddenly became interested in the brightly decorated bottle that now sat in the middle of the table.

"When did I agree that we were going to tell everyone about this?" Anton reprimanded him.

"What's the big deal?" Johnno seem amused by Anton's antics.

"You could have at least consulted with me first."

"Just remember I was the one who found it," Johnno snapped at him.

"Yeah, well who was the person who stubbed their toe on the piece of driftwood huh?" Anton countered. "If I hadn't tripped over it to begin with, you would never have even seen the bottle."

"Yeah, well you can keep your piece of wood. The bottle is mine!"

"The bottle is ours," Anton corrected him.

"Umm, excuse me," the waitress interrupted them. "Are you two going to read the letter or shall I?"

The two boys stopped their squabbling and stared at the bottle that stood in the middle of the table. Somewhere during the course of their argument the waitress had simply picked up the bottle and pulled out the cork while waiting for them to finish deciding who found it first. It now stood silently between the two cups of coffee while she held the cork up for both to see.

"Maybe the two of you should learn to share," the waitress said matter-of-factly, bringing the argument to an end.

"You're right," Anton said. "You found it Johnno, so technically it's yours. But it's just a letter so maybe we can both read it together instead of squabbling over who found it first. After all, we're best friends remember."

"I guess so," Johnno agreed. "I mean it's probably just a silly letter from some young girl. We'll read it together."

"That's better," the waitress said, satisfied that she had solved the problem. "There's just one more thing. Can I read the letter when you're finished? I'm a huge sucker for anything romantic."

"I suppose so," Johnno said. "I mean. There's no harm in that is there Anton?"

"That's fine dude. It's your letter."

"Our letter," Johnno corrected him.

"Okay I'll leave you two alone then," she said. "Just wave me over when you're done. I'm Kim, by the way."

"It's nice to meet you Kim. I'm Anton. Obviously you're a new face around here because I come here most mornings and I haven't seen you before." Anton extended his hand which she shook politely. However she never once looked his way. All the while her eyes were trained firmly on Johnno's.

"Hi," was all Johnno could manage to say at first as he took in her warm smile. Finally he swallowed back the lump that had caught in his throat and followed it with, "I'm John."

Anton counted to ten while he watched his friend's face glaze over. He seemed transfixed by the sight of the pretty Asian waitress who did nothing but continue to hold his hand while she brushed a strand of her black hair back behind one ear. Finally he snapped his fingers three times and the two returned to reality.

"Excuse me. Hello!" Anton shook his head in disbelief. "Are we going to read the letter or shall I leave the two of you alone and come back later?"

"Pleased to meet you John," Kim laughed as she gently let go of his hand. "I'll come back when you and your friend have finished reading your letter."

"I'd like that," said John.

7.05am

My wish to you

"What was all that about?" Anton looked across the table in disbelief at his friend.

Johnno was still watching Kim as she walked across the timber deck floor and disappeared through the doors of the café. His eyes had fallen to her black hair that swayed pleasantly back and forth across her shoulders. Johnno remained mesmerized by the sight of her even when all he could see was her head as she worked busily behind the counter inside the building.

"Johnno!" Anton shouted at him in a subdued whisper.

"What?"

"The waitress?" He hissed at him, still amazed by the sudden transformation of the love struck fool who now sat across from him. "I mean really? You've never even met her before. And what's with this John nonsense all of a sudden? You hate being called John."

"That's not entirely true," Johnno turned to face him again.

"Yes it is."

"My mother calls me John."

"Well I hope you don't look at your mother the way you were just looking at her!" Anton screwed up his face at the thought. "So where does this leave you and Tanya?"

60

"What about her?"

"Come on. You know." Anton leant across the table so that his voice didn't attract any attention. "All that stuff you said about her before, how you like her curvy figure."

"I never said that!" Johnno said defensively. "It's just, you know, I mean... I admired the way she was confident about her body shape, that's all!"

"So where has this sudden interest in Asian waitresses come from?"

"She's different, that's all."

"In what way?"

"She doesn't hate me like Tanya does." Johnno tried to change the conversation. "Can you let it go now? I thought we were going to read the letter."

"Okay," Anton agreed as he put his hands up in surrender. "If that's what you want dude. I've only been trying to get your attention for the past ten minutes. So who's going to read it first then?"

"We'll read it together," Johnno said as he moved the chair around the table so that he was next to Anton.

Johnno grabbed the bottle and turned it upside down. The letter caught in its neck. Then with a bit of prying using his car key, he was able to gently pull the letter from the bottle and let it fall onto the table. It lay there wrapped only with a small hair ribbon tied in the center. Anton reached across to untie it as Johnno stood the now empty bottle back in the center of the table.

"Well here goes." Anton said as he uncurled the two pages and held them up for his friend to see.

The pages were cream in color, decorated with a border of flowers entwined along the edge of each page in black ink. At the top of the first page before the letter began, was a small turquoise colored love heart someone had painted, again in what appeared to be nail polish. It left a slightly oily stain around the edges which only added to the letter's charm. Around them, the air filled with the scent of women's perfume that wafted up from the page. With their curiosity now firmly aroused, Anton and Johnno huddled in closely and began to read.

To whoever finds this,
If I've washed up on your distant shore,
From a land far over the sea.
Please tread carefully on the morning sand,
And know you've set me free.
Wrapped in my mother's ribbon,
This letter is but a token.
A plead to let her see the world,
From a young heart torn and broken.
A turquoise heart that was my Aunt,
Left footprints in the sand.
Her magic just a memory,
You now hold in your hand.
So I light a candle for my Dad,
But this gift I give to you.
He always told me to make a wish,
So today may all yours come true.
It's time to live, to find true love.
Before the winter's scorn.
Somewhere it's always summer,
May my true love's arms be warm.
P.S. Please return me to the sea at sunset.

"Whoa, what do you make of that?" Johnno asked the moment he finished reading.

"I think it's beautiful. So meaningful and deep, like the ocean," Anton sighed. "I want to read it again."

"I knew you'd like it," Johnno snorted. "It's a bit too lovey-dovey for my liking though. What's on the other page?"

"Nothing. It's blank," Anton said in disbelief as he held the two pages in his hands.

"Are you sure?" Johnno asked, as though there was a chance Anton may have missed something.

"See for yourself." Anton passed the blank page to him. "I think perhaps we're meant to write something on it. You know, before we pass it on."

"Like what?"

"Oh I don't know. Like greetings from Kings Beach or something."

"Do you think it's just a little girl somewhere having some fun?" Johnno thought for a moment.

"Well she had to be old enough to buy the bottle of wine," Anton tried to reason. "The handwriting is beautiful, too neat to be a young girl, and of course there's the perfume."

"So what do you think?" Johnno asked him keenly. "Do we get a wish?"

"I'll tell you what I think. I think she's beautiful," Anton sighed pleasantly. "I can't believe I'm saying this dude, but I think I'm in love."

"What?"

"It's true. I've been looking for someone like this all my life." Anton waved the letter in front of him as though to prove his point. "I don't care what she looks like. She has an inner beauty that just floats off the page like a heavenly scent. I think that she's real, and she's out there somewhere."

"So what are you going to do?" Johnno looked at him dumbfounded. "Do you think you can find her?"

"I don't know," Anton shook his head. "This could have washed to shore from anywhere. Do you think we could wish her here?"

"Are you kidding?" Johnno looked at him sternly. "We don't know how many wishes we get and you already want to waste the first one on finding whoever wrote this? What if it's just one wish Anton? What if we only get to make one wish? I really think we should consider this carefully."

"Yeah of course," Anton agreed with him. "In fact I think we should be very careful with even using the word wish until we find out if this is the real thing. But even if it's not, I'm going to find the girl who wrote this letter."

"So what are we going to do now?"

"I don't know." Anton for once appeared lost for words.

"Great. What a morning this has turned out to be then," Johnno sighed as he slouched back in his chair. His eyes drifted once more to where Kim stood behind the counter. "It seems I'm obsessed with an Asian waitress and you're in love with a genie in a bottle!"

7.10am

Wishing for Scrambled Eggs

Tanya watched the boys curiously from inside the kitchen as she prepared to bring them their breakfast. They had been acting strangely all morning, and she hated the thought that the two were talking about her behind her back. Still she wondered if perhaps she had been a little too hard on Johnno this morning. She just found it infuriating how easily he managed to claw his way inside her inner-psyche and push buttons that she didn't want pushed. Not until she found the right man to marry. And Johnno, she continued to remind herself, was definitely not the right man!

Still it bugged her that she didn't know what they were talking about. They were like two old witches huddled around the table, talking secretively and conspiring to hatch their evil plan. She glanced in their direction again, convinced now that they were definitely talking about her. Probably pointing out all of her flaws to each other and making fun of the fact that she was a size fourteen and didn't look good in a bikini like the bevy of other beauties that paraded around the beach. Well how would they like to be in her shoes? They didn't know what it felt like to squeeze into a skimpy bikini and have everyone judge them on how they looked. Instead men got to hide their saggy bottoms in a pair of board shorts. Well for once, just once she'd like to see Speedos come back into fashion for men and see how they like it!

The thought made her smile. Suddenly the bitterness subsided and the happiness she had felt this morning returned. It was her birthday, and last night she had made a promise to honor the memory of her parents and her Aunt by vowing to forge ahead in her pursuit of happiness. After all, this was the new version of herself. The new Tanya was going to cast aside all of her bitterness and no longer spend her life hiding behind the pages of a diary. She would float free with the tide and see where life would take her.

Perhaps that had been her problem all along. Last night had finally made her aware that living her life in memory of her parents was only making her feel miserable. Her parents had been strong Christians their entire lives and had raised her as every strong Christian parent would. She still went to church every Sunday and sat and worshipped amongst people who were strangers to her every other day of the week. She was still a virgin waiting for God to introduce her to Mr Right.

It had only occurred to her this morning that she was nothing more than a naive little girl. Until last night she had no idea what dating meant in the mind a non-Christian. Sebastian had known she was a Christian. But did he really know what it meant to *be* a Christian? Had she failed to explain to him that being a Christian meant more than simply saying that you believe in God? Or had a part of her grown tired of waiting for God to introduce her to the right man?

It scared her when she woke this morning that she found herself wondering how last night would have ended had she not slapped Sebastian across the face. Not that Sebastian was the right man either, but maybe she would be basking in the warmth of beautiful confusion this morning instead of wallowing in the indignity of having no-one to love. It only made her wish her mother was still alive to talk to about how she felt.

As soon as the boys' order was ready, Tanya carefully picked up the two plates and stepped out of the kitchen. She told herself to stop being silly. Being a virgin at twenty-six was not a curse. There was still time to find Mr Right, and no-one was talking about her behind her back. She'd known Anton and Johnno for a long time now. There was simply no way that Anton would ever have a bad word to say about anyone, especially her. It was time to hand the problem over to God. It was the only way she would be able to leave behind the guilt she felt burdened with from being reminded of her parent's death every time another birthday rolled around.

Johnno could see Tanya inside the café. It looked as though their food was finally on its way.

"So are you absolutely sure of this?" He asked Anton.

"I'm positive," he reassured him, still holding the letter. "It says right here, '...This gift I give to you, he always told me to make a wish, so today may all yours come true.' Don't you see what she's done? I'm pretty sure she's talking about a birthday wish, only her wish was for all of ours to come true. It has to be more than one wish dude!"

"Okay Anton. I'm going to trust you on this one," Johnno said, trying to stop himself from shaking as he prepared to put the theory to the test. "But I still think we start out with something small okay? I don't want to change the history of the world or do anything stupid."

"Sure," Anton agreed with him. "What are you going to wish for then?"

"How about this for starters?" Johnno looked at him excitedly. "I only ordered two slices of raisin toast remember?"

"Yeah. So what?" Anton looked at him puzzled.

"Well, what if I wish for sausages and scrambled eggs on toast?" He beamed proudly.

"Oh yeah. That's a good one," Anton said excitedly. "That sounds safe enough for our first try until we figure out how this all works."

"Here she comes now," Johnno said. "Try to act normal."

Tanya stepped out of the café and onto the sprawling timber deck that spread out to the footpath that overlooked the beach. In each hand she balanced the two plates the boys had ordered and the cutlery wrapped in individual paper napkins. Stepping beneath the branch of the huge pandanus tree that adorned the front of the café, she made her way to the table that Anton and Johnno occupied and set the plates down in front of them.

"Here you go," she said routinely as she placed the cutlery down beside each plate. "Two of the sausage with scrambled eggs on toast, enjoy."

"No way!" Anton exclaimed as he stared at the plate in disbelief.

"I'm sorry. Is there a problem?" Tanya stopped and stared at the two boys who looked like they were in shock. When neither of them answered she began to grow worried. "Anton, you're starting to freak me out a little. Is everything okay?"

"It's sausages and scrambled eggs!" Johnno said loudly as he stood to his feet. "Sausage and eggs, can you believe it!"

"No way dude!" Anton whistled. "It worked, it actually worked."

"What worked?" Tanya asked him sternly. "What's going on with you two this morning? You haven't been acting yourselves from the minute you walked in here."

"It's just that Johnno ordered the raisin toast," Anton said matter-of-factly.

"I'm sorry," Tanya apologized. "I must have grabbed the wrong order from the kitchen. My head was a million miles away. I can go and find out what happened to your order if you like. Otherwise you're welcome to have this for no charge."

"No it's fine," Johnno reassured her as he sat back down, "the eggs are fine."

"Anton, what's really going on here?" Tanya pulled up a chair and sat down opposite the two boys. "I'm not leaving until you explain to me why you are both acting so weird."

Johnno looked nervously across at Anton who then nodded his head silently and pulled out the letter for Tanya to see.

"We found this on the beach this morning," Anton said quietly. "Apparently we've been granted the power to wish for whatever we like."

"It's true," Johnno spoke up. "I wished for sausages and scrambled eggs and it came true."

Tanya's face went pale with shock as she first recognized the letter, and then the opened bottle in the middle of the table. The same bottle she had decorated with all the different shades of nail polish she possessed in her collection. The letter written on the pages she had torn from her diary and poured her heart onto. She had hoped that today was going to be more than just the beginning of another day, and here they were making fun of her.

"Hey you read the letter, what did it say?" Kim asked as she too pulled up a chair and joined the other three at the table.

"It was a poem," Johnno said. Once more he seemed intoxicated by the very presence of the sultry waitress.

"Ooh a poem. Is it romantic?" She asked, moving in closer to Johnno who now held the letter for her to see.

"She knows about it too?" Tanya asked. A look of embarrassment spread quickly across her face that luckily wasn't noticed by any of the other three.

"You should read it Tanya," Anton said excitedly from across the table. "We we're going to show you once we'd finished reading it. But you are not going to believe how deep this girl's thoughts are. You can tell simply by the way the words float off the page. Honestly you'll have to read it for yourself. It's beautiful."

"I can imagine," she fumed quietly.

Tanya watched the three as they fussed over the letter. Fascinated at the same time by the apparent chemistry that had sprung from virtually nowhere between Johnno and the new waitress. Only then did it occur to her. No-one suspected it was her. In their own naive eagerness to embrace the idea of the letter actually being magical, they had all failed to recognize that the person responsible for writing it was sitting at the same table. She quickly hid her fingernails from view beneath the table. The others had failed to notice that they were painted in the same beautiful shade of turquoise that matched the love heart she had painted on the letter.

She smiled secretly at the thought of their childish excitement. Surely it was just a simple mistake on her behalf when bringing Johnno his breakfast that now had them convinced that the letter was going to make all their wishes come true. Or was it in fact a strange coincidence that they had tested their theory by wishing for scrambled eggs. Surely she couldn't have created magic. Surely this was all a coincidence.

Either way, she was going to have a little fun with them!

7.20am

This obviously isn't working

"**W**ish for something else," Kim said to Johnno excitedly.

"Like what?" Johnno asked before hungrily stuffing another helping of egg into his mouth. He was not only excited at the thought of having the power to wish for whatever he wanted, but also at the thought of a girl actually being interested in him for once.

"Oh I don't know, anything," she said mischievously. "Diamonds, handbags, expensive watches."

"No, we have to think about this for a second," Anton said firmly. Deciding to take control of the situation before it got out of hand. "There obviously has to be some rules, some kind of understanding of what we're dealing with here. Otherwise we could be altering the history of the world, impacting the environment, forever changing the shape of the universe."

"Would you listen to yourself?" Kim snapped at him impatiently. "It's just a little fun, how is a Prada handbag going to affect the universe? Ooh, that's a good one! Wish for one of those for me John."

"John?" Tanya spoke up, suddenly confused. "Since when have you started calling yourself John?"

"It's a long story." Anton winked at her. "I'll fill you in later."

ot work," Anton said dejectedly. "I don't understand."

"Maybe you said it wrong," Kim said quickly. "How did you make your wish before?"

"Yeah, think carefully Johnno." Anton's mind was already turning over a thousand thoughts.

"When you wished for the sausage and scrambled eggs, how did you say it? What words did you use exactly?"

"I said I wish for sausages and scrambled eggs on toast," he replied. "The next thing I know they just appeared."

"You could wish for anything you wanted and you wished for scrambled eggs on toast?" Tanya asked him in disbelief. "Oh that's just great."

"Try again then," Kim still sounded upbeat, trying hard to build up John's confidence. "But think really hard about it. Say it like you mean it."

"I wish for a Prada handbag!" He shouted unnecessarily.

"Go on." Kim nudged him. "Be more specific."

"I wish I had a little black and white handbag with dangly things!" He shouted once more.

Again nothing happened.

"I wish for a black and white Prada handbag with silver trinkets!" He finished shouting at the sky.

"Oh please!" Tanya smirked. "Will the three of you listen to yourselves? This is ridiculous, it obviously isn't working."

"Hey pretty boy!" Someone shouted from a group of surfers

72

who were sitting four tables away. "Maybe your boyfriend will get you one for your birthday."

"Sit down Johnno," Anton whispered loudly to him. "You're embarrassing us."

All across the timber decked dining area of the café, every eye at every table was now firmly trained on them. The four sat there red faced for a moment, soaking up the silence uneasily until finally the gentle banter of conversation resumed and they drew a collected sigh of relief.

"Who were you talking to, God?" Anton jibed his friend. "And what's with all the shouting, you think he's deaf too?"

"No, it's just that..."

"Do you know what this means?" Anton cut him off in mid-sentence. "It doesn't work when you make a wish for any material possessions."

"How can you be sure?" Kim asked. "Why don't you try making a wish then?"

"Okay, I will." Anton stopped to think for a moment. "Just to prove to you all that I am right."

"Go on," Kim encouraged him. "This is so exciting."

"I wish that a black Mercedes-Benz C-class convertible would suddenly appear in the parking lot."

"Oh please, this is just getting silly," Tanya mocked them. "This whole scenario that you have going is just ridiculous. I obviously made a simple mistake with your order Johnno, that's all. In fact there's more chance of you having magic eggs on your plate than that letter having the power to grant you wishes."

On cue, in the parking lot in front of the café, a black Mercedes-Benz convertible pulled into one of the empty parking spaces. The four turned as one, with mouths opened in stunned silence, and watched as the doors opened. A couple in their early fifties got out and walked inside the café, locking the doors behind them with the remote. Their eyes then fell to the handbag that rested over the shoulder of the well groomed lady. It was black and white with silver trinkets dangling from the handle, and most important of all it was Prada!

"It worked!" Kim giggled excitedly as she clapped her hands.

"You have got to be kidding me!" Tanya looked at them all angrily as she got to her feet. "It was a coincidence, that's all. What are the three of you going to do now, go over there and rob that sweet couple of her handbag and steal their car? I can't stay here any longer and listen to this. I've got work to do. I suggest that you join me Kim or we are going to have the manager coming over here and kicking our behinds. There's a small crowd building over at the counter."

"Oh alright then," she sighed as stood up. "You sure know how to spoil all our fun."

Tanya just glared at her menacingly. Although she thought she could have a little fun with the letter at the boys' expense, the longer she listened to all their nonsense the more it annoyed her. Writing the letter was supposed to make her feel better, and somehow watching the other three treat it like a carnival sideshow only caused her anger to rage inside. There was something more to it however, something else lying below the surface that didn't feel right. It had something to do with Kim being involved. The girl had only been at the café for a little over a week and here she was making herself the center of attention in something that was supposed to be a turning point in her life.

Tanya turned to see if Kim was following her back to the counter. Instead she was leaning closely over Johnno, gently stroking his arm and handing him a piece of paper that must surely have had her phone number scrawled on it. Suddenly it occurred to her what had really been bugging her all morning. It had sprouted up from a tiny seed in her heart, growing like a thorny vine until finally it had reached the point where it was choking her. It was jealousy. Kim was making her move on Johnno.

"Kim!" She called sternly, drawing the attention of more

than just the pretty twenty something Asian waitress. "We've got customers."

"So I'll see you this afternoon?" Kim continued to flirt with him. "About four o'clock?"

"Sure, I'll be here." Johnno stared into her dreamy eyes. "I'll see you then Kim."

"Goodbye John," was all she said before smiling once more and walking towards the counter where Tanya stood waiting.

Johnno watched as she floated inside the café. Oblivious to the total look of disapproval that Tanya was throwing in his direction. If he looked closely, he would have been able to see the steam rising from her ears as she reached boiling point. Yet all Johnno was capable of focussing on once more was the pair of legs that carried away the most amazing girl that he could ever have wished for.

"Hey Romeo. Have you got a minute?" Anton asked as he finished his breakfast.

"Yeah. What's up?" Johnno asked, turning back around to face his friend yet unable to hide the huge smile that had spread across his face.

"I think you might have made Tanya a little mad by distracting Kim from her work," he said and motioned subtly with his head in the direction of where she still stood glaring at the two.

Johnno turned to look at her and their eyes locked. At that moment he became scared that she might actually walk back over and slap him across the face. He could feel her anger radiating like the heat off the surface of the parking lot on a hot day and he had to look away.

"Man, did you see how mad she looked?" Johnno sighed as he squirmed uncomfortably in his chair. "I told you she didn't like me."

"It's alright she's gone. It's safe to look again," Anton said once he was satisfied that she had made her point and had safely returned inside. "I think she might be a little mad at the both of us."

"Yeah, well I wish she liked me," Johnno sighed. "It's kind of uncomfortable when she's in one of her moods."

"It's not your fault dude. I think she just chooses to take it out on you for some reason," Anton said quietly.

"I know," Johnno agreed. "I always try to be nice to her but it seems like it's nothing but a waste of time. Honestly mate if it wasn't for the two of you being such good friends I wouldn't have anything to do with her."

"Don't worry about it," Anton's face lightened up. "We've got more important things to take care of this morning. Like how to work out the secret to this letter."

"I don't know Anton," Johnno sulked. "I know we all got caught up in it before, but do you really think it's going to work? I only ended up looking stupid."

"I don't think Kim thought you looked stupid," Anton said as he playfully punched him on the shoulder. "That's real cool dude. You only just met her and you've already got her phone number and a date this afternoon."

"It's not a date. I'm just meeting her after work," Johnno blushed.

"Work?" Anton suddenly sat upright. "Dude, it's nearly quarter to eight!"

"Oh no, I'm going to be late for work!" Johnno almost fell out of the chair trying to get to his feet.

"No, you're already fifteen minutes late."

"I wish I didn't have to go to work today," he said as he tried to hide the sound of rising panic in his voice.

"I wish you didn't have to either dude." Anton said. "The surf's really pumping and we've still got to figure out how to make this letter work, so why don't you just wish for the day off?"

"Yeah right," Johnno scoffed. "While we're at it why don't I wish I was someone famous on TV? I'll tell you why. Because it's not going to happen."

"So? Just call in sick or something."

"I can't mate. The project is running behind schedule and the boss has really been riding everyone's case lately." Johnno stopped to look at him and the color almost drained from his face. "What am I going to say? I'm going to be half an hour late."

"Say you had car troubles," Anton suggested. "It always works for me."

"Yeah but you don't have a job," Johnno sighed with frustration. "You don't even have a car."

"Well you don't have to tell everyone," Anton laughed. "Are you still sure you don't want to take the day off?"

Johnno hated how everything just seemed like a big joke to Anton. It was bad enough that he was late for work. Now he was getting job advice from a man with no responsibilities, a man who in society's eyes did nothing. The truth was that construction on the apartments was coming to a close. Very soon the final fit out would be complete and the job would be over as far as the laborers were concerned. Johnno had to hope that he'd hear word soon from the construction company of when and where their next job would be. So long as the site foreman didn't have a bad word to say about him, he'd then have another project that would see him through the next six months.

"I've got to go," Johnno said firmly. "If you want your surfboard from the back of the van then you'll have to come and get it now."

"No, it's alright dude. I'm meeting Sebastian here at half past nine," Anton answered smoothly. "That should fill in some of the morning. My board can stay in the van ready for our surf this afternoon but I'll grab my backpack from off the front seat."

"You're still meeting with the writer guy every week?"

"Sure am," Anton answered as he stood to his feet and followed Johnno out into the parking lot. "You know how it goes, sitting around and bouncing ideas off each other over coffee."

"No, really I don't."

"Then I've got that so called unemployment review meeting at the social security office. And I'm guessing it wouldn't look too good if I walked in there with my surfboard under my arm."

"That's today?" Johnno asked quickly.

"Sure is. I've been looking forward to it like a trip to the dentist," Anton laughed. "Oh, and don't forget there is that meeting with Mal at the holiday park this afternoon."

"That's this afternoon? But I'm meeting Kim here at four o'clock."

"Relax dude. The meeting is at half past three." Anton yawned and stretched his arms out above his head. "There's plenty of time to do both."

"How do you fit all of this in?" Johnno looked at him in bewilderment. "For someone who is supposed to be out of a job you sure keep yourself busy."

"I try."

8.00am

I wish I knew

"Let me guess, he had to leave in a hurry or he was going to be late for work again," Tanya said smugly as Anton sunk into one of the comfortable lounges inside the café.

"Hey, however did you know?" Anton replied sarcastically.

Outside the sun was beginning to bite. Even the sparse shade of the tree was not enough to stop its scorching advance. So like he did most mornings, he moved inside. It was also a chance to kill some more time, change the scenery, read the paper and wait until the breakfast rush was over so that he could talk some more with Tanya.

"You know what?" She stopped in front of the lounge where he sat and looked him firmly in the eye. "I blame you."

"You blame me?" Anton said sheepishly. "You cannot be serious. What have I ever done that could possibly make him run late for work?"

"You're a bad influence Anton," she began, "if it wasn't for you he wouldn't be surfing before work, forgetting to bring his work boots or wasting the whole morning on a letter in a bottle you found washed up on the shore."

"Why are you being so nice to him all of a sudden?" He stopped to ask her and the thought that instantly sprung up in his mind had his breath catching in his throat. Hadn't Johnno wished for Tanya to be nicer to him only a few minutes ago? Could this really be happening? It had to be he thought. In all the years he'd known Tanya, he'd never once recalled her having a nice thing to say about his mate Johnno or rushing to his defense like she was now.

"I wish I knew," she sighed before shrugging her shoulders and swatting at an incessant fly that had been buzzing around her face.

"Hey, where'd your friend go?" A now familiar voice suddenly asked.

Anton looked up to see Kim standing beside Tanya. Her broad smile and chirpy voice was in complete contrast to Tanya's solemn look of despair. His mind made the connection the moment he saw the two girls standing beside each other. It took all he had inside of him to contain the look of shock from the realization of what had truly been bugging Tanya all morning. Any thoughts of wishes coming true were forgotten for the moment. This was something far bigger. This was something huge!

"Oh, Johnno had to go to work," Anton said proudly. All the while he kept one eye on Tanya's facial expression to see if it would change. "You know how it is. He's working on this big project. It's a massive construction actually and he had to go and check on some of the structural engineering issues. You know, to make sure the boys were following the plans correctly."

"Ah. Sounds exciting," Kim purred. "That explains why he looks so big and strong."

"Well he also works out a lot," Anton said as he watched the tiny furrow lines appear on Tanya's brow. "Yeah, he sure is a fitness freak. You know, healthy lifestyle, healthy mind, that kind of thing."

"Wow, he sounds like a really great guy," Kim smiled.

"Yeah, did I mention that he's single?"

"I already gathered that much," Kim blushed, "I'm meeting him here this afternoon remember?"

"Oh, yeah right." Anton tried to act forgetful while at the same time noticing that Tanya's lips were now pursed tight together and knowing that he was definitely onto something. "I wasn't paying all that much attention. John and I are very respectful of each other's space. I guess it's because he's such a sensitive and caring kind of guy."

"Oh he sounds wonderful," Kim quickly caught her breath. "Since you're his friend, can I ask you something?"

"Sure Kim, what is it?"

"Do you think he'd find me too forward if I asked him out on a date this afternoon? It's just that he's obviously so shy and sensitive and I don't want to wait forever for him to ask me out."

"I don't think he'd mind at all Kim," Anton answered her, still watching Tanya as she neared boiling point. "The poor guy has been all work and no play lately. I keep telling him he has to get out more if he wants to meet women, but you know John. He's not into the nightclub scene or anything like that. He once told me that he'd somehow just know when the right girl comes along."

"What do you think Tanya?" Kim giggled with excitement. "Isn't he just the dreamiest thing you've ever seen on two legs?"

"I suppose so. Now if you'll excuse me I've got some things to take care of in the kitchen," she said quietly as she turned and hurried away from the table.

"Excuse me for a moment Kim," Anton apologized as he stood to his feet. "I've um, just got something I need to take care of. I'll talk to you later."

"That's alright. I've got a customer that's just walked in anyway," Kim said. Although it was obvious that she was watching curiously as Tanya disappeared into the kitchen.

Anton followed Tanya into the kitchen not knowing what to expect. He had pushed and pushed, hoping for a reaction that would give him the answer that he needed. Now that he had it, he didn't quite know what to do next.

"Tanya," he said carefully as he stepped into the kitchen.

"What are you doing back here?" She seemed surprised as he gently stepped around the chef and walked towards her. "You're not supposed to be in the kitchen, you'll get me in trouble."

"I know what has been eating you up this morning," he said.

The room fell into complete silence.

Tanya stood in the middle of the galley, feeling the eyes of both Anton and the chef trained firmly in her direction. Finally she sighed aloud and brushed a strand of long, blonde hair back behind her ear.

"I'll give the two of you some privacy," the chef interrupted. He put his apron down on the bench, suddenly feeling uncomfortable with being caught in the middle of something he knew nothing about. "Make it quick though, I've just put on some more sausages and scrambled eggs."

Tanya waited until he had left the kitchen and turned to face Anton angrily.

"What is it Anton?" She tried not to yell at him. "What is so important that you feel the need to march in here and tell me what my problem is like you're my psychiatrist?"

"Oh I think you know what I'm talking about," Anton confronted her. "But are you going to admit it? Or are you just going to keep playing this little charade of yours and watch Kim end up with what you really want instead?"

"Admit what?" She tried her best to answer bravely, but only failed. Instead she found herself choking back the tears.

"That you're in love with Johnno."

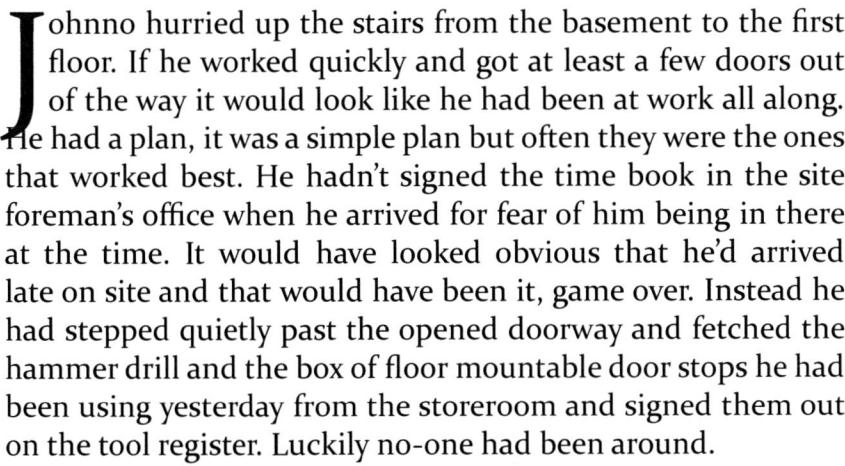

8.15am

Never saw that coming

Johnno hurried up the stairs from the basement to the first floor. If he worked quickly and got at least a few doors out of the way it would look like he had been at work all along. He had a plan, it was a simple plan but often they were the ones that worked best. He hadn't signed the time book in the site foreman's office when he arrived for fear of him being in there at the time. It would have looked obvious that he'd arrived late on site and that would have been it, game over. Instead he had stepped quietly past the opened doorway and fetched the hammer drill and the box of floor mountable door stops he had been using yesterday from the storeroom and signed them out on the tool register. Luckily no-one had been around.

Now if someone stopped him and asked where he'd been all morning, he could say that he had been held up in the storeroom signing out everything he needed for the day. If they checked, they'd see that he'd signed for the tools at seven-thirty. Later of course he would find the site foreman and tell him that he forgot to sign the time book when he arrived this morning. The foreman would check the tool register, see that he'd signed out tools at half past seven and be satisfied that everything was as it should be. It was a small lie, but it was a perfect plan, provided that he could get enough doors finished in time.

Johnno bounded up the last few steps two at a time, reaching the door of the fire escape that spilled out onto the first floor. The construction site was beginning to look more like a finished block of apartments rather than the giant hole in the ground it had resembled eight months earlier. Of course he had only begun working on site once the building had reached the stage where it resembled a giant, hollow concrete shell. That was when the carpenters and laborers would move onsite and begin to fit out each of the apartments.

There were only two apartments on this floor and if he moved quickly he could be up on the second level in around twenty minutes. Pausing near the doorway, he shifted the weight of the box in his arms, opened the door slightly and peered out. Thankfully there was no-one there. Slipping into stealth mode like a character in a video game, Johnno stepped out into the hallway and hurried down it until he reached the first apartment. Once there he closed the door behind him and began to set up.

It didn't take long to measure where each doorstop was to go. He drew out a rough template using a piece of cardboard from a discarded box of floor tiles that one of the tradesmen had left behind and set about his work. The sound of the impact drill soon roared to life as the drill bit hammered its way through the dusty tiles and went deep into the concrete floor. Johnno repeated the process a second time until he had two perfectly aligned holes. Working faster than a pit crew on a race car, he then proceeded to change the drill bit for a Phillips head screwdriver attachment, whacked in two plastic screw lugs with a hammer and then held the doorstop in position while driving home the two screws.

Moving from door to door, he quickly repeated the scene several times. There was no time to check the plans. Thanks to that other fool he worked with that was always checking on him, the site foreman probably thought he was already up on the fourth level by now.

Once the first apartment was finished, Johnno had to hurry the full length of the first level to reach the second apartment. His mind was too busy with other thoughts as he moved quickly to even notice that the entire level was deserted. Instead he breezed into the next apartment, closed the door behind him and set about repeating the scene all over again.

As he slipped into a rhythm Johnno found his thoughts reflecting on the morning so far, from finding the message in the bottle after a perfect morning of surfing, to thoughts of the cute Asian waitress he was going to meet again this afternoon. He'd never had a girl seem this interested in him before and it seemed strange territory to be sailing into. If the letter in the bottle really did have the power to grant his wishes, he most probably would have ended up wishing for a beautiful woman to be his girlfriend. Surely though that would not have compared to the thought of knowing that someone was actually interested in him. Wishing for a beautiful girl was one thing, getting her to fall in love with you was something altogether different. Was it even at all possible to wish for somebody to love you? He honestly didn't know the answer to that one. Over the course of two years he hadn't been able to get Tanya to even like him, so he didn't know what chance even a genie would have of making someone love you.

As soon as the first level was finished, Johnno gathered his tools and hurried back down the corridor to the nearest fire escape, throwing the door open and disappearing into the stairwell again just before a voice called out from the other end of the hallway.

"Who's there?" It shouted helplessly as Johnno failed to hear it and disappeared into the shadows.

Johnno in his own panic was so focussed on the task of fitting as many doorstops as he possibly could before the site foreman eventually caught up with him that he didn't hear the voice. He just continued to leap the stairs two at a time until he reached the second level and threw the door open. He saw the open door on the apartment to his left and disappeared inside, quickly closing it behind him.

Wrestling with the crudely made cardboard template, Johnno quickly set the drill bit back in place and proceeded to sink two more holes into the concrete floor. The dust again found its way up into his nose, just like it always did. So he responded once the holes were finished by placing a finger to one nostril and blowing until a gray booger flew out and landed on the dirty tiled floor. After tapping the plastic lugs into the holes, he changed the drill attachment and again rammed home two screws. There was just enough time to gather his tools and move clear of the front entrance before the door swung open and a police officer with his gun in hand stormed into the apartment with the site foreman right behind him.

"Put your hands where I can see them!" The officer shouted, causing Johnno to drop the power drill and the box he held in his hands. They crashed to the floor where the box split open and the doorstops tumbled free.

"Johnno, what on earth are you doing here?" The site foreman shouted at him in amazement.

"I was just working," Johnno answered nervously. His hands were now visibly shaking. "I'm sorry I was late for work but please don't shoot me!"

"It's alright. You can put the gun down. He's one of ours," the site foreman instructed the police officer and Johnno found himself thanking God that the man obeyed.

"This site is strictly off limits," the police officer said sternly. "You had no business to cross a police line and unlawfully enter a crime scene."

"What crime scene? What are you talking about?" Johnno asked, still confused as to what was happening.

"Honest son, you must be the biggest fool alive to have

walked through all the yellow tape surrounding the building," the site foreman said before shaking his head in disbelief. "Did it even occur to you that there was no-one on site?"

"So no-one's here?" Johnno asked.

"Of course not. I had to send everyone home," the foreman grunted. "If you had been here on time this morning then we wouldn't be having this conversation right now would we?"

"As I said, this is a crime scene now," the police officer reminded him once more. "There was a fatality here this morning, the scaffolding on the west side of the building gave way and a man fell to his death. We're treating it as suspicious. I'm going to have to ask you to leave the premises immediately, or I'll be left with no choice but to forcibly remove you or take you into custody and charge you with trespassing."

"It's alright," the site foreman put the officer at ease. "I've got this one covered. After that you can do what you want with him."

Johnno looked blankly past the site foreman at the officer who only smiled mischievously in his direction and slowly nodded his head.

"Clark, you're fired!" The words rang loudly in the empty apartment. "Now get your things and get off this site."

"Look I'm sure this is a simple misunderstanding," Johnno protested. "This is just an innocent mistake that could have happened to anyone."

"You really think so?" The site foreman said looking at him in disbelief. "By turning up today you've only given me the chance to do what I was going to do tomorrow anyway."

"I don't understand what did I do wrong?" Johnno tried to plead with him.

"See those doorstops that you spent all yesterday drilling holes and mounting to the floor?" He pointed to the mess scattered at his feet.

"Yeah, I finished all the fire escape doors in the stairwell before I went home yesterday, just like you asked."

"Oh you did?" He asked smugly. "So you would have checked first to see which doors already had stops mounted to the rear of the doors?"

Johnno went blank while he tried to remember if he even checked the back of the doors at all. In his haste to get as much work done as possible he had simply hurried between floors, drilling holes as quickly as he could and mounting them *all to the floor.*

"Just as I thought," the site foreman barked at him. "I don't even want to hear an explanation as to why half of my stair doors have two doorstops on them. We have plans to follow for a reason and some of those doors required the stops to be mounted on the back of the doors and others required them to be mounted on the floor."

Johnno looked despondently at the back of the apartment door that he had just finished. It too had two doorstops, one on the floor and a second one on the back of the door.

"Can't you at least give me another chance?" Johnno pleaded, secretly hoping that there still might be a way he could avoid losing his job.

"I'm afraid it's too late for that," the foreman scoffed at the thought. "You see it isn't up to me. You also failed to sign the time book when you left yesterday. When the project manager went through the time book this morning after the accident, there was only one other person that we couldn't safely account for being off site. You! That's a breach of the site's safety policy son. That's a cause for instant dismissal."

"So that's it? I'm fired," Johnno answered his own question. He could sense now that there was nothing further that could be said to change his mind. To be honest, he would much rather leave now with his tail between his legs than stand here for a couple seconds more and take the brunt of the site foreman's frustration. "Well in that case I guess I don't need to be standing around here listening to anymore of this."

"You've got that right son," the foreman continued. "I've already wasted enough of my time on you this morning."

"Yeah, well I shouldn't have even bothered coming to work this morning." Johnno snapped back. "I've never liked working for someone who is so..."

"Okay, that's enough let's go." The police officer stepped forward and grabbed him by the arm, dragging him past the visibly irate site foreman and into the hallway outside.

"I wish you never stepped foot on my site son. You've been nothing but a thorn in my backside!" He yelled at Johnno as the police officer escorted him off site. "I'll see to it that you never work in this industry again. You are without a doubt the worst employee I've ever known!"

"Yeah, well you wouldn't even recognize a good worker if one fell out of the sky and hit you on the head!" Johnno shouted over his shoulder as the police officer dragged him down the hallway.

"I hate to be the one to break it to you son, but you didn't exactly fall out of the sky this morning now did you," the site foreman only laughed at him.

"Well... Well, I wish something would fall out of the sky and land on you." Johnno countered lamely. "It might finally knock some sense into you."

"That's enough. Now let's go," the police officer said firmly as he led him away.

8.30am

That's how I feel

"**W**hy haven't you been able to say anything about this before?" Anton asked Tanya the moment she joined him at the little table tucked away deep inside the café.

"Because every time I found myself thinking of him in that way it would only make me more annoyed," she groaned. "What is wrong with me today Anton? I've known Johnno for almost two years and in all that time I've been nothing but mean to him. I'm rude to him every time I see him. I treat him terrible and the moment someone else is interested in him I'm ready to pull her hair out and go crazy!"

"Ah, jealousy my friend," Anton sighed as he settled back in the chair. "It strikes when you least expect it and fuels itself on the anger that burns inside. You stoke those flames hot enough and then boom! You've got yourself a blazing inferno and no chance of putting out the fire."

"What am I going to do?" She looked at him despondently. "You're my friend. I can talk to you about this kind of stuff, right?"

Anton stopped and thought about that word. What really was the meaning of the word friend anyway? Was friendship nothing more than a barrier stopping someone from telling another how they truly felt about them? A curse bestowed on someone who has feelings for a member of the opposite sex they can't really share for risk of ruining the friendship?

Anton had known Tanya for a long time. Way before Johnno had arrived on the scene. He remembered striking up a conversation four years ago with a young, twenty-two year old waitress who had just moved up from the city. She had dreams similar to his of one day wanting to travel the world. She also believed in never letting life bring you down but rather learning to enjoy each day for what it was. So as their conversations became more regular, Anton started dropping by the café purely to see her rather than buying coffee. Then one day she had dropped the 'f' word, and there it had sat uncomfortably ever since.

"Yeah, of course you can." Anton snapped his mind back to the conversation at hand. "You know that, right?"

"I'm so glad to have a friend like you." She placed her hand gently on his arm as it rested on the table.

Anton felt his heart skip a beat. The same way it had on countless other occasions when she had drawn close to him or brushed past him. It momentarily sent a shiver up and down his spine. It was moments like these that he simply couldn't deny the feelings he had for her. Though he kept them contained, holding them back like an ocean of emotion, they were always lurking and waiting to surge forward like the changing tide. There was only one girl that he had ever truly loved, and it was her. Only she didn't know it. Now he sat across the table from her, poised to give advice on what she should do about her feelings toward his best friend. He thought it was time to stop holding back the sea.

"Have you ever had times when perhaps you've thought of me in the same way?" He asked, feeling the butterflies rise up from his stomach. "It's just that I can't sit here anymore without first telling you how I feel about you."

Anton felt the earth stop turning as the words just dangled there in the silence. All that he could hear was the hiss of air brakes releasing from a garbage truck as it came to a stop outside the café. Beneath his feet he could imagine the thunderous rumbling of cogs in a huge piece of machinery as they ground to a halt. He felt the weight of the universe that was about to collapse in on him. Strangely enough he could even sense that the tide was about to turn. As Tanya continued to sit opposite him with her mouth wide open, he knew that something had just completely changed.

"Um, Tanya," Anton said as he placed his hand over the top of hers. Finally her eyes snapped out of their dazed state and focused on his. "If there's anything you want to say, now would be the time to do it."

"I don't understand," she said quietly. Still letting the sudden change in their conversation sink in. "What exactly are you trying to say Anton?"

"I'm in love with you Tanya," he said calmly. "I have been ever since I met you."

She quickly pulled her hand out from under his and in that moment Anton realized he had stepped over a line she had never intended him to cross.

Finally, there was the answer to his question. What was the real meaning of the word friend? It was a person that was well known by another. It was someone who is liked and regarded as loyal. It was an ally, a supporter, someone you could trust. It was someone who is on the same side. Looking across at Tanya he realized that they were now on more than opposite sides of the table. They had taken opposite views of each other over the one thing that was capable of breaking down any barrier, love. If friendship was a barrier to love, it now seemed that love was a barrier to friendship.

"Look Anton," she finally gathered herself together and answered him sweetly. "I like you very much, but only as a friend."

92

There was the 'f' word again.

"That's alright. I understand," Anton answered quietly, but unable now to look her in the eye.

"Hey it's okay. If anything I think it's very sweet." She reached out to gently touch his hand, but her advances only caused Anton to slowly get to his feet.

"Oh you poor thing. Are you going to be alright?" She immediately felt terrible.

"I just need to go for a walk, that's all."

9.00am

This can't be happening

"Have you seen Anton?" Johnno said in desperation the moment he burst into the café.

"I think he's just gone for a walk to clear his head," Tanya said. Puzzled as to why Johnno was here and not at work. "He said he was coming back though. I think he's meeting Sebastian at about nine-thirty."

"Oh right, the writer guy."

"Yeah. What's up Johnno? Why aren't you at work?" She asked, still wondering what was so important that he had to leave work to come looking for Anton.

"It's that letter we found this morning," Johnno said. "Now I know you're going to think I'm stupid, but I think the wishes we've been making might actually be coming true."

"Are you sure?"

"At first I wasn't," he admitted. "But now I'm one hundred percent sure!"

"Are you sure it's not just a coincidence?" Tanya began to feel uneasy with the thought of her heartfelt poem turning into something more than just a touch of niceness to brighten up somebody's day. "How can you be so sure?"

"There, look on the TV!" He shouted as he pointed to the television that was mounted on the wall inside the café. On it were pictures being beamed from the construction site that he'd just come from. "Can we turn the volume up on this thing?"

His sense of urgency attracted some onlookers who also turned to look at the television. Johnno jumped up on the lounge chair beneath it and turned the volume up.

"Oh my goodness. That's here in Kings Beach," Tanya said as she walked nearer to the screen. She then stood quietly beside Johnno, whose eyes were already glued to the news report.

"Hi John. I didn't expect to see you this early," Kim's chirpy voice interrupted when she caught sight of the pair standing in front of the TV. She raced over to join them. "Why are you back so soon?"

"Can you be quiet for just a second Kim?" His voice was abrupt and instantly caused her happy smile to disappear from her face.

"...Police are still treating the accident as suspicious and have not ruled out sabotage as the cause of death for one unlucky construction worker earlier this morning when a section of scaffolding on the west side of the building gave way, causing the worker to fall from the eleventh floor."

"Hey, that was you I just saw on TV!" Tanya exclaimed as the camera scanned the scene. For one brief moment it focussed on the image of Johnno leaving the construction site.

"Ooh John. This makes you famous now you're on TV," Kim said as she moved in closer to put an arm around him.

Tanya watched quietly and could only try to hide her disgust.

"Wait, it gets worse," he sighed.

"...In another completely separate incident this morning, a second man believed to be the site foreman who had been helping police with their investigations was injured when a rent-a-loo that was being removed from site by a crane suddenly gave way. The portable toilet that was being raised by crane to allow detectives' clear access to the scaffolding fell and rolled over on top of the man after a chain broke. The man was rushed to

hospital where it has since been reported that he is receiving treatment for minor injuries. Our cameras were filming when the incident took place shortly after eight-thirty this morning and we warn viewers that the following pictures may be disturbing."

"Good grief!" Tanya winced as she watched the replay of the rent-a-loo as it fell from the crane. "You were there when it happened?"

"I'm afraid it's much worse than that," he sighed sadly. "I wished for it to happen."

"You can't wish for something like that to happen," Tanya said in disbelief. "It's just not possible. You can't deliberately make your mind will an unfortunate accident to occur. It's a coincidence that's all."

"It's the same as the eggs Tanya," he moaned. "Remember? All I had to say was I wish for sausages and scrambled eggs and the next thing you know they appeared."

"This is not scrambled eggs we're talking about here Johnno," Tanya tried to reassure him. "You poor guy. You're taking this all to heart aren't you? Look Johnno, it wasn't your fault okay. You have to understand that. All of this happened because of the toilet man, crane operator or whoever it was that they showed on the news. Not because of you."

"You don't understand." Johnno paused to rub his forehead, feeling the grief well up uncontrollably inside of him. "I'd just lost my job, and..."

"You lost your job?" Tanya tried to console him. "Oh you poor thing, here come and sit down and I'll get you a cold drink. We're going to talk about this okay. I don't want you feeling that you have to take the blame for this."

"*I'll* get you a cold drink John," Kim said as she glared jealously at Tanya. "What would you like?"

"Is an iced-tea too much trouble?" He asked tentatively as he sat down on the lounge chair beneath the television. He could sense the two girls staring coldly at each other.

"That's no problem at all," Kim said sweetly, breaking her stare with Tanya.

"That would be great," he thanked her.

"You stay right there," she commanded before turning to look accusingly at Tanya once more. "I'll come back and then we can talk, unless of course you'd prefer to talk to *her!*"

Johnno could feel the tension in the air. It was so thick between the two girls that he could feel it wrapping around him like a boa-constrictor, squeezing the air from his lungs. He didn't know what was going on. If the girls were having a fight with each other before he'd arrived, then he wished they didn't take it out on him.

"I've got to find Anton and tell him," Johnno said as Kim glided across the floor to the front counter.

"You're not going anywhere," Tanya said. Her voice sounded soft and soothing as she sat down beside him on the couch and began stroking his head gently. "Anton will be back shortly and you can talk to him then. Right now I want to make sure you're okay."

Johnno turned and stared at her in disbelief. She was actually being nice to him! In fact she was being more than just nice. She was now stroking his head affectionately.

"Alright you can stop that now," he said as he stood to his feet.

"What's wrong?" Tanya asked innocently, staring up into his big, brown eyes while gently biting her bottom lip.

"You're being nice to me."

"Of course I am. What's wrong with that? You've been through a lot this morning and I just want to make sure you are okay."

"The problem is you're never nice to me. In fact I've always thought you hated me."

"I don't hate you Johnno," she corrected him sweetly while tugging on his hand and hoping he'd sit back down. "I'm sorry if I've given you that impression in the past, but maybe it's just me seeing you like this that has made me realize just how much of a nice person you really are."

"No it's not," he shrugged her reasoning aside. "You're only being nice to me because I made a wish for you to be nice to me."

"You made a wish for me to be nice to you?" She asked in disbelief.

For a moment he thought the old Tanya might break free and reach forward to strangle him. It flickered somewhere deep in her eyes and then it was gone.

"Yes I did. And somehow it came true," he said growing more animated by the second. "You've never been this nice to me. Can't you see what's happening? It's the letter. Whoever wrote it obviously bestowed some kind of magical power on it. When I said I wish for sausage and scrambled eggs, they suddenly appeared. So I wished that I didn't have to go to work today and then I find out there was an accident and they'd sent everyone home. Not that it mattered because apparently I was going to be fired anyway. So I told the foreman I wished something would fall out of the sky and land on him and whammo!"

"You can't be serious. The rent-a-loo?" Tanya asked in disbelief.

"That's right. Do you see some kind of pattern forming here? I've got to find Anton and sort this out right now. Otherwise we've got no idea where this is going to stop."

"Don't go," she pleaded with him. "Please stay here and wait for him. It's not the letter Johnno, I really do like you."

"I've have to go. Tell Kim I'll see her later," he said quickly before hurrying out of the side entrance and leaving her alone on the lounge.

Tanya sighed and sunk back into the chair. The morning was growing more complicated by the minute and now she'd have Kim angry at her for letting him leave. She closed her eyes and tried to make it all go away.

"Hey where did John go?" Kim said as she returned with the iced-tea.

"He's just gone to try and find Anton," Tanya replied uncomfortably. Feeling guilty that Kim had already noticed her open display of interest towards Johnno. "He said to tell you he'd be back later."

"You better not have said anything to make him leave," she said accusingly. "I saw how you were looking at him before."

"Hey ladies," the chef suddenly interrupted their squabble. "You don't get paid to lounge around and drink iced-teas. Now I don't know what exactly is going on here this morning but it's going to stop right now, *comprendre?* I'm not covering for either of you if the owner stops by and sees you sitting around while there are customers waiting at the front counter. Oh, and another thing while I'm here. What's with all the orders for sausages and scrambled eggs? I've got three orders sitting there in the kitchen and no-one seems to know who they are for."

9.15am

What are the Rules?

Anton had been sitting on the sand not far from the café when he first caught sight of Johnno bounding across the sand in his direction. At first glance he thought there was no way that it could have been him. Johnno would have been at work. Another cog in the machine that was society, plugged into the system, nose to the grindstone while working on some high rise building that wasn't needed. All so that more holiday makers could escape the city for two weeks of the year and find their solace by the sea. As he drew nearer however, there was no mistaking the awkwardness of which he plowed his burly frame across the sand. Feet kicking up clouds of sand in their wake, arms flailing as though he was trying to maintain his balance and face straining as he demanded his body to keep up, because as far as Anton could remember, Johnno never ran.

"Anton!" He called as he neared where Anton sat calmly watching the surfers who were still cutting their moves across the remaining morning swell. "Anton I'm so glad I found you."

"Hey Johnno what's up?" He asked, watching in amusement as his friend dropped to his knees in exhaustion. "Did you change your mind about taking the day off dude? You know, come back one last time to chase the endless summer."

"No, it's important," Johnno puffed between words,

exhausted from the hundred yard sprint across the soft sand. "Something's happening man, we've got to work out what to do about this letter."

"What do you mean dude?" Anton looked at him astonished. "Weren't you the one who thought it didn't work? If I recall before you left in such a hurry this morning you said it only made you look stupid."

"That was before," he sighed as he flopped onto the sand beside Anton. "Everything's changed man. The letter is real."

"So what happened that made you change your mind?" Anton's interest peaked.

"Everything that we've wished for this morning is beginning to come true," he said as he finally began to catch his breath. "It started out innocently with the eggs. But so far this morning I've had a gun pointed at me, I've been fired from my job and now Tanya is being nice to me. Not just nice, nice, but *really* nice. I haven't had much time to think about it, but whatever we wish for comes true. Sometimes not instantly, but sooner or later in some indirect way it comes true."

"Whoa! Slow down for a second. You had a gun pointed at you head?"

"I sure did. I even caught a glimpse of myself on the news."

"Okay, tell me everything from the start." Anton shook his head in disbelief. "What happened from the moment you left the café?"

"Remember how I wished that I didn't have to go to work?"

"Yeah of course," Anton hurried him along. "Just tell me why you're here and not at work."

"It turns out there was an accident this morning on site. Someone fell to their death from the eleventh floor. Everyone was sent home. Only I was late for work, somehow managed to walk across a police line without noticing it and ended up with a police officer pointing a gun at me."

"What on earth for?" Anton almost shouted.

"Apparently they are treating the whole thing as suspicious," he stopped only to draw a breath. "Luckily the site foreman was with him at the time and explained everything to the police officer. But unlucky for me he also had a bee in his bonnet over me being late and fired me!"

"I guess you lucked out on that one."

"I know." Johnno shook his head, still coming to terms with the fact that he and Anton now shared something very much in common, they were both unemployed. "Only it gets worse. Naturally I'm pretty much angry by now, so as the police officer is dragging me off the building site I turn and shout at the site foreman that I wished something would fall out of the sky and land on him."

"What happened next?" Anton asked eagerly.

"It was nuts! Everything happened so fast, I mean there was a television crew there covering the accident from earlier that morning and they were filming me as I was leaving the site..."

"No way!"

"Yeah, I saw myself on TV at the café only a few moments ago," Johnno said as he grew more animated. "So as I'm leaving the site I hear someone yell '*look out*'. I turn around just in time to see this crane that had been lifting a rent-a-loo up onto a flatbed truck that was parked beside me suddenly have one of the chains give way. The toilet crashed to the ground and then tipped over and landed right on top of the site foreman!"

"No way!" Anton said as he pondered the irony. "Did he die?"

"No, but he is in hospital," Johnno said in disbelief. "It may only turn out to be minor injuries but still, I didn't mean for that to happen to him."

"But you are saying that you wished for something to land on his head, and in a way that's kind of what happened right?"

"That's right," Johnno groaned. "But I thought it would only be something like a bird-poop landing on his head. Not a rent-a-loo."

"So what did you do then?"

"After that I drove to the café looking for you, only you weren't there. So as I was explaining what had happened to Tanya and Kim, Tanya starts acting all nice to me."

"Maybe she was just feeling bad for you dude. After all you'd just lost your job."

"That's what I thought too man, but then she started stroking my hair!"

"She was stroking your hair?" Anton asked in disbelief, remembering his conversation with Tanya in the kitchen only a short while before.

It had turned out that Tanya had feelings for Johnno from the very first moment she had met him. Not the fanciful feelings a girl gets when she notices the first sign of attraction to a particular man. Rather a deep yearning to pursue his affection at all costs. She wanted this to be *the* man. The one and only who would ask her hand in marriage and ride blissfully off into the sunset together. Only the thought scared her to death. Apparently the whole Christian thing meant she stood the chance of being rejected on two completely different levels. One if she mentioned how she felt about him and two if she shared her love of Jesus. And so to keep her feelings under control she tried desperately to push him away at every opportunity. As far as Anton could tell it had worked. Until today when she realized that she had ultimately pushed him into the arms of another woman.

"So I was right," Anton mused quietly.

"What do you mean you were right? I've got a problem here man. I think she's flirting with me," Johnno sighed from the weight of it all. "I know I wished that she'd like me. It's just that I have this thing going with Kim now, and she was trying to be affectionate with me in front of her at the café. She can't do that. It's going to ruin everything. I finally meet a girl who likes me and then this happens. I get two girls behaving jealously over me, and one of them only because I made a wish for her to like me. We've got to be careful about what we wish for!"

Anton didn't know whether to tell Johnno a little of what Tanya had confided in him earlier. To do so would be to admit that he too had feelings for the brown eyed blonde he had risked losing a friendship with. Unless Johnno felt the same way about Tanya, who was he to interfere? Of course he knew all too well that Johnno did like Tanya, at least up until he had met Kim this morning. So what if by saying nothing at all he was allowing his two best friends to ultimately end up with the wrong person? This was getting confusing. Instead he tried to focus on the letter.

"Okay, there must be some kind of formula that the letter is following," Anton thought for a moment. "Can you recognize any pattern that is forming from anything that we've wished for this morning?"

"All I can come up with is that it somehow seems like a coincidence each time it happens," Johnno sighed.

"You're right," Anton agreed. "It seems the letter only provides the means necessary for whatever we wish for to happen. That's why everything seems to be happening as though it were a coincidence. Notice anything else?"

"Well, it seems to work regardless of whether it's you or me making the wish." Johnno said curiously.

"Okay, so it grants power to the person or persons who find the bottle." Anton said.

"What about Kim though?" Johnno suddenly asked. "Wasn't she the one who actually opened the bottle?"

"Yeah you're right," Anton thought carefully. "I guess until we can figure out whether it's the act of finding the bottle, opening it or reading the letter that is granting us the power to make a wish, we'll just have to be careful. I'd hate to think of what Kim would be capable of wishing for if she discovered it worked for her also. What else can you think of?"

"Well strangely enough whenever we've talked about what we've already wished for nothing else happens."

"Yeah you're right," Anton said. "Perhaps it doesn't apply to anything mentioned in the past tense. I don't know if that also means we can't un-wish anything that has already happened, but from here on we should be careful with any wish we make. Everything we've wished for has only happened when we've started the sentence with the words I wish."

"What about the Prada handbags then?" Johnno asked. "I must have wished for half a dozen of them and they never materialized. "Maybe we can't wish for objects."

"Not necessarily so," Anton's face lit up. "The eggs turned up and you ate them didn't you? Then there was that old woman who arrived in the black Mercedes. Didn't she have a handbag exactly the same as what you wished for? I think what was really wrong dude was the way you made your wish. You said I wish for a Prada handbag, not I wish I had a Prada handbag. There's a big difference between the two."

"What about all the others though? Shouldn't there have been more than one handbag appear?"

"Yeah you're right," Anton replied. "Maybe we never waited around long enough to see if more than one would appear. I think we can both agree that whatever we wish for doesn't necessarily appear straight away. For example, if I say I wish that a busload of gorgeous beach volleyballers would appear right here on the beach, it doesn't mean that they are going to appear out of thin air. They have to be real which means they have to come from somewhere. For all we know they're getting on the bus right now but who knows how long it will take for them to get here. See what I'm saying dude?"

"Yeah I do," Johnno smiled. "Do you realize that you just wished for a busload of gorgeous beach volleyball players to come here?"

"Yes my friend, I believe I did." Anton grinned with delight.

"I think the rules are, be specific, be patient, but most of all be careful what you wish for."

"What happens now?" Johnno asked, eyes scanning the beach for any sight of a group of girls playing beach volleyball.

"Now my friend we learn to have a little fun and see just what this day is really capable of." Anton patted him on the shoulder as he stood up and grabbed his small backpack which also contained the letter and brightly decorated empty bottle. "Right now I've got to go and meet Sebastian. But stick around, do some surfing and enjoy your day off. Just make sure you come and get me when that bus arrives."

9.30am

Is that handbag Prada?

Anton walked through the front doors of Mermaids and immediately caught the attention of Tanya who was working behind the front counter. The day was turning out to be a hot one already. He could tell by the fact that the staff were now content to loiter inside the café that the air-conditioning must be working wonderfully. As he passed under the giant blower that was suspended above the doorway, he felt a cool rush of air wash over him that caused his fresh t-shirt to dance across his shoulders like it was still pegged on the clothesline in the morning breeze.

Somewhere during the course of the morning he'd slipped into the change rooms by the parking lot that overlooked the beach and had showered and changed. Although the change of clothes had done nothing to disguise his presence as he slipped quietly into his usual seat perched above the front counter that looked straight out to sea. Tanya was beside him like a shadow the minute he slid along the red vinyl lounge behind the table and dropped the small backpack he had been carrying onto the floor beside him.

"Where have you been?" She demanded before he even had a chance to look up at her. "Johnno's been looking for you and I had no idea where you went after you left here earlier."

"It's alright. He managed to find me," Anton replied coyly, still unsure where their friendship sat in light of what he had said before.

"I wanted to see you before Sebastian got here," she said as she sat down beside him. "You know, to make sure everything is okay between us."

"Why wouldn't it be? We're still friends, right?" He tried to remain upbeat as he answered her, but a touch of hurt still lingered on the edge of his voice.

"What I wanted to say is that you took me by surprise before. That's all," she said softly. "We've been friends for four years now and I guess I've never thought that you might have feelings for me in that way. It's all very sudden for me. The whole morning has been so weird. Firstly with Johnno falling for the new girl Kim, and then me admitting that I have feelings for him. All I wanted to do this morning was get my head around my date with Sebastian last night before he walked in here and further complicated the matter. Then there is you, the bottle, the letter... you."

"Of course, you and Sebastian." Anton immediately felt guilty for not asking earlier how it had all gone. "So it was a date, not just dinner?"

"Uh-huh."

"How did it go?"

"I slapped him."

"That bad huh?" He winced as he pictured her slapping Sebastian. "Are you okay?"

"I'm fine," she sighed. "It wasn't because of anything that he did wrong. It was me. I realized when he kissed me that he wasn't the man I wanted to be kissing."

"And that man would be Johnno, right?" Anton asked.

A simple nod of the head was all he needed to know where they stood.

"Hey, it's alright." He stood and put his arms around her.

"You can tell me. That's what friends are for remember."

"So you're not just saying this to make me feel better?" She looked up at him.

"No not at all," he said as she let her head rest on his shoulder. "I think you're the most wonderful person I know. A friendship with you that could last a lifetime is far better than any romance that has no guarantee."

"So you're still coming to my birthday party tonight?"

"I wouldn't miss it for the world," he said as he gave her a little squeeze.

"Well that certainly makes me feel a lot better," Tanya said as she looked him in the eye and smiled.

"Oh, I almost forgot to give you this," Anton said. He reached under the table and grabbed his backpack. Unzipping it he took out a small, brightly wrapped present and handed it to her. "Happy birthday Tan."

"Thank you Anton," she smiled warmly as she took the present in both hands. "You could have waited until tonight."

"I wanted to give you this now," he replied, suddenly wishing he could take back what he'd said earlier this morning. Perhaps it was only natural when you were such good friends with a member of the opposite sex to wish there could be something more than just friendship.

"Should I open it now?" She asked as she sat down and placed the gift on the table.

"Of course," Anton said as he sat down beside her.

Tanya delicately pulled back the wrapping paper and held it up for him to see.

"Nail polish. Oh Anton they're beautiful." She smiled genuinely despite the fact that he had forgotten to take the seven ninety-five price tag off the small gift box containing three bottles of nail polish in almost identical shades of pink. She knew all too well that in Anton's simplistic lifestyle it probably amounted to a lot of money.

"I remembered you telling me the story of your Aunt giving you nail polish for your sixteenth birthday, so I thought you might like a nice reminder."

"Thank you Anton. You're such a good friend," she said sweetly and gave him a quick kiss on the cheek.

And there it was again. The 'f' word.

"Well I hope you like them," he said casually, finding that the word settled between them a little more easily now.

"I do. In fact I'll wear one of them tonight to my birthday party."

"Right, the party." Anton put the whole episode of this morning behind them. "Is Sebastian still coming?"

"I hope so," she said nonchalantly. "Although I can't picture Sebastian being able to accept the idea of just being friends like you are able to. So now you'll understand if I excuse myself and go look busy before he gets here."

"Right," Anton nodded in agreement. "There's a prime example of a romance without a guarantee."

"It sure is," Tanya said quietly as she reflected on last night's date with Sebastian. "Although I wouldn't call it a romance, it was more likely a dinner that ended awkwardly."

"I can see where you're coming from," Anton sighed as he stretched his legs under the table, in the process kicking something with his feet.

"I'm glad we've got that clear," she smiled innocently in return. "I would have hated for us to end up that way. I feel too embarrassed now to be in the same room as him."

"Hey, what is it that I keep kicking under the table?" Anton appeared momentarily distracted while he quickly reached down and came back up clutching a small black handbag. "Someone's left their handbag behind."

"Is that Prada?" Tanya reached across the table and snatched the handbag from him.

"What's a Prada?" Anton asked curiously. "It just looks like a handbag to me."

"It's only the most expensive handbag on the face of the earth," she gasped as she saw the gold insignia stamped on the side. "It must belong to the lady who was here this morning in the black Mercedes."

Anton looked across the table at the girl holding the Prada handbag. The girl who wore the same colored nail polish as the love heart that was drawn on the letter he had found this morning and finally he made the connection. It was Tanya who had written the letter. She had tragically lost both her parents and her Aunt, just as the girl in the poem had described. And she was the one who should be making her birthday wish today. *If only she hadn't passed the wish on to whoever found the bottle!*

Anton tried to hide the smile on his face. Tanya had known all along. From the moment they had opened the bottle over breakfast this morning she had kept the fact that she had written the letter a secret from the group, but why?

Perhaps he too would keep his knowledge quiet for now, until he found out whether this was all purely a coincidence.

9.50am

Shadow of an Author

Sebastian Wolsey strode into the side entrance of the café with the air of importance usually reserved for the likes of visiting dignitary or officialdom. Certainly not fitting for a local rental agent whose desk was tucked away in the corner of some obscure realtor in the main street of town. Unless of course you happened to be *the* Sebastian Wolsey. Not only the former bestselling author of *Road to Nowhere*, but the author once quoted as being the most promising new voice in literature that this country had seen in years. Despite the drubbing his second novel had received in the press, he still considered himself to be somewhat of a local celebrity. Even if that meant quietly accepting a job as a rental accommodation agent when his publisher had torn up his contract after... Well let's just say *that* book.

Sebastian spotted Anton talking to Tanya in the usual seat that he occupied every Wednesday morning. It was the same table that had become increasingly hard to commandeer throughout the summer school holidays. Thank goodness the hordes of families that had choked the beach with their sandcastles, striped towels and beach umbrellas all summer long would soon go back to the city he thought. Perhaps then life would return to normal.

He could do without the sight of overweight Dads in Speedos pretending they were someone important for choosing to take their family to the trendy café rather than simply buy their kids an ice-cream from the guy in the ice-cream van in the parking lot. All they succeeded in doing was making a mess by dripping water all over the floor before finally leaving a big, fat, wet reminder of their visit on the chairs when they left. Well good riddance to them he thought before nearly slipping on the wet tiled floor. Sebastian waved his arms awkwardly and tried to regain his composure. Any air of importance that he'd floated in on had now flown right back out the door. The wet sand beneath the soles of his black leather shoes grated loudly, and only made him grit his teeth with annoyance. It seemed some things never changed.

He'd hoped he may have a moment to talk to Tanya alone. After all he couldn't understand what on earth he had done wrong last night. He'd recognized very early that Tanya was the type of girl who liked to take things slow. So he hadn't rushed her into making any decision in the twelve months he'd spent pursuing her. She was intelligent, she was strong minded, but more importantly she was one of those religious-types who still held on tightly to some very old-fashioned morals when it came to men. And he thought he'd made a pretty good effort of showing her that he respected that.

Right now however he could see her sitting beside Anton and opening what looked like a birthday gift. Sebastian stopped and watched from where he stood hidden from view on the lower level of the café, beneath a giant framed poster of his second book he had signed for the owner. It still hung proudly on the wall behind the espresso machine.

Sebastian couldn't tell what it was that she had unwrapped. All he saw was her lean in and kiss Anton tenderly on the cheek. The sight of the two together only made him feel numb. Had that been the problem last night? Was there someone else? It had to be the reason. Why else would she have slapped him simply for an innocent kiss? Looking at the two of them together it all became clear. Tanya and Anton were an item. He had no idea how long they had kept it a secret. After all, he thought the two were only friends. So why would she have agreed to go out for dinner with him? He'd spent a fortune on her at the most expensive restaurant in town, and for what?

He was about to turn and walk out of the café when he noticed Tanya was on her feet again. If she saw him leave now it would probably only make the situation more difficult to deal with. He thought it was best to face up to her and apologize again for last night. Maybe then she would at least have the decency to tell him the real reason for her behavior.

As he walked up the steps to the upper level he thought he caught a glimpse of Tanya looking in his direction. But before he could be sure that she'd seen him, she made a sudden detour into the kitchen and was gone. Rather than call out to her Sebastian simply pretended he hadn't seen her.

"Hey, Sebastian. Sit down and take a load off," Anton called out cheerily at the sight of his friend walking towards his table, and slapped the seat beside him noisily with his hand. "Top of the morning to you dude."

Sebastian brushed unnecessarily at the striped, designer label shirt he was wearing despite it already looking immaculate. He always seemed to dress in complete contrast to the usual crowd of beachgoers that frequented Mermaids. Not only did he stand out dressed in freshly pressed black trousers, Italian shoes and a long sleeved shirt when the temperature outside the café was already pushing into the mid-eighties, but his piercing blue eyes cut an imposing presence from under his stylish, short black hair.

Sebastian quickly eyed the confines of the café before lazily sliding into the seat beside Anton. He didn't know who he was looking for in particular. What was more commonplace these days, clients or fans? The truth was he hadn't been asked for his autograph since a book signing late last year at the little bookstore in town on top of the hill. On that day he'd only sold four copies.

"How's things today Anton?" Sebastian greeted him wearily as he slouched down behind the table. "It's getting hot outside, that's for sure."

"Isn't it just a great morning?" Anton sighed while looking out the window at the endless surf that was still pounding the shore. "It's the kind of morning that wakes you up like a slap across the face with a cold fish. Man, its days like these that make you question why anyone would want to live anywhere else."

"I'm sorry if I'm not in the mood for superlatives Anton. I've just come from a so-called meeting at the office," he groaned. "What is it with people that they can't understand the difference between peak season and off-peak season? Honestly we're fully booked this week. One hundred percent capacity, not a single room to spare and I get some joker from the city ring up this morning wanting accommodation for tonight. One night I tell you. He thought he'd just come up for a drive and stay the night. Sort of a spur of the moment thing and can't understand why I can't find him a room."

"Tough morning huh?" Anton listened intently, hanging off every word he said. "I was wondering why you were a bit later than normal."

Sebastian was somewhat of a hero to Anton. The man was able to look past his shabby dress sense and the social stigma of being unemployed and see someone who was more than just a fan. He made Anton feel as though he was on a level playing field with him. He appreciated his insight, his poetic approach to the ordinary and the one thing they shared very much in common, words.

"Tell me about it. But it's not like you had anywhere else you needed to be right?" Sebastian asked as he took a quick glance at the expensive watch that dangled from his wrist and totally ignoring the fact that he was twenty minutes late. "Anyway, not only does this joker want to give me a spray of verbal diarrhea, but when I get off the phone the manager tries to give me the third degree about why I couldn't persuade him into making a booking for next week. So far next week we are below forty percent occupancy. The summer's over and everyone would rather be back at work instead of enjoying the beach when it's nice and quiet."

"That's the nature of the beast," Anton sided with him. "It's a bit of a one in all in thing I suppose. Otherwise they'd all be here next week to book the same room for half the price."

Sebastian didn't know how he came to be drawn into the circle of friendship with someone the likes of Anton. Here was an unemployed poet who lived in a trailer park with generally no prospects of becoming anything greater than what he already was. Yet somehow he maintained a way to be happy with his situation. It fascinated him and scared him a little at the same time that perhaps he was looking at his own fate. With his fan base shrinking, book sales plummeting and little or no respect left from within the publishing industry, he was forced to throw himself into a fulltime job again to provide a secure income. Even if it was only a temporary measure he reminded himself until he got his career back on track. Anton seemed to fill the gap that existed between fame and obscurity perfectly.

"What I don't understand though is why?" Sebastian struggled with the concept. "It's the same room next week as it is today, only with a change of sheets and a different date."

"Ah, but you're missing the point," Anton leaned forward with eyes lit up. "For the simple reason my friend that it is summer. It's the time of year when everyone wants to spend their days getting sun-burnt, watch their ice-cream melt all the way to their elbow and generally enjoy having sand kicked in their face at the beach. The sort of things you can't put a price on."

Sebastian gave a slight chuckle and seemed to snap out of his mood, at least temporarily. At work he may only be Sebastian Wolsey, rental agent. But whenever he was with Anton he transformed back into Sebastian Wolsey the author. It was one of the reasons he continued to meet with him every Wednesday at the café. Not just any café but Mermaids, the café from which he borrowed the name for the title of his second book, '*Swimming with Mermaids*'. At least Anton had understood what he was trying to do by writing the book in a completely different style to his first.

"Hey, was that Tanya I saw you with as I came in?" Sebastian asked. "If she's around I might order us all a cup of coffee."

"I think she's around somewhere," Anton replied coyly. "She's been busy helping out in the kitchen all morning."

"Oh well. I might get one of the other waitresses to take our order," he sighed disappointedly. "I was hoping to at least say hello to her after last night."

"Yeah I've heard it didn't go all that well for you man. I'm sorry," Anton offered.

Sebastian stopped to look him squarely in the eye. Was his so-called friend going to sit here and pretend like nothing happened? After all, he'd seen the two of them together only moments before when she had kissed him. There was only one way to find out.

"I want to ask you something Anton, and I want the honest truth when you answer. Okay?"

"Yeah sure," Anton replied almost a little too casual.

"Is Tanya seeing someone else?"

"Why would you ask that?" Anton looked at him curiously.

"It seemed that last night at the end of our date there may have been someone else on her mind when I kissed her."

"I heard."

"I don't care if you heard," Sebastian tried not to sound menacing. "I want to know if there is someone else that she is interested in besides me."

Anton felt himself pressed into a difficult situation. On one hand he felt he owed Sebastian an explanation for Tanya's behavior last night. On the other he couldn't really say anything about Tanya's feelings towards Johnno. He hadn't even had the right opportunity to discuss the matter with his best friend. All the while Sebastian was staring him down, waiting for him to say something, anything.

"All I can tell you Sebastian is that I think it took a date with you for her to realize exactly who she should have been on a date with," Anton tried to answer delicately. "Don't take it personal man. It wasn't anything to do with you, and I'm sure Tanya was going to let you know once she had sorted out how she felt."

There was the answer Sebastian had wanted to hear. He took a moment to study the look on Anton's face and thought it best not to press the man for any more of an explanation. It had to be as difficult for his friend to tell the truth as it was for Sebastian to hear it. Still it angered him that he had more to offer Tanya than the few meager possessions Anton had to his name.

"Hey, how's the new book coming along?" Anton asked.

Sebastian tried to cheer himself up by the thought that Anton was still interested in his writing. Only it wasn't working. His work colleagues thought they were better than him simply because they possessed a real estate certificate that he did not, and now it seemed so did his friend because he had the girl that Sebastian so dearly wanted to call his own.

"I'll tell you how the new book is going," Sebastian became irrational. "It's going terribly, horribly wrong."

"It is?" Anton seemed surprised. "Just last week you said you had thought of a way around the character conflict in chapter twenty."

"I thought I had," Sebastian continued. "Only now I realize

that I've wasted the past twelve months in pursuit of a character I thought was going to determine the outcome of the story!"

"This is still about Tanya isn't it?" Anton slouched back in the lounge chair.

"In some ways I guess it is," Sebastian said coldly. "If I hadn't wasted the last year pining after a girl I thought was interested in me, then maybe I would be in Alaska right now writing my third novel. Instead I'm stuck in some nine to five job with people who look down on me for daring to try and achieve something they themselves are not capable of. I'm up to my eyeballs in debt and my agent this week suggested I try someone else to represent my work in the future."

"That's too bad," Anton tried to console him. "Is there anyone else you can try to pitch your next novel to?"

"Oh, so now you have all the answers for my problems?" Sebastian snapped at him. "Maybe I should trust your judgment and it will all work out for the better."

"Hey Sebastian, what's really wrong here man? This is me, Anton. If there is something that's bugging you why don't you just tell me?"

"Do you know how much it costs to buy a two bedroom log cabin on five acres of pristine, remote riverfront Alaskan wilderness with year round road access?" Sebastian rattled the question off as though he had asked it a thousand times before.

"No, I wouldn't have the faintest idea," Anton seemed puzzled by the question.

"Forty-nine thousand dollars," he answered without taking his eyes off Anton.

"I don't understand." Anton wondered how they had gotten off the subject of Tanya and onto the topic of real estate prices in Alaska. "What point are you trying to make?"

"The point is most people would spend quite a few thousand dollars on a thirty day Alaskan holiday, something that I have been putting off for the past year," he began, "and for what purpose?"

"I honestly don't know Sebastian, but I wish you'd tell me what is really going on here."

"Alright, I'll tell you what is going on. I've put my life on hold for the past year, working the same stinking job that is barely covering my mortgage payments in the hope that I might actually have a chance with Tanya. Now as it turns out that chance is gone and I'm sitting here listening to you tell me that she realized only last night that there is someone else she has been interested in this whole time." Sebastian slapped his forehead in frustration. "Do you have any idea how that makes me feel?"

"No, honestly I don't man," Anton countered him. "But for once I wish you'd make up your own mind about what you want to do with your life instead of trying to blame everyone else for every little thing that goes wrong."

"Right now I'd be better off selling my house, clearing all my debts, and buying that log cabin in Alaska. At least I could move there with some money in my bank account, make a fresh start and finish writing my third book. Besides, why should I stay here now that you've taken Tanya out of the picture for me?"

"So you think I'm the one she's interested in?" Anton asked in disbelief.

"Oh come on," Sebastian leant back in the chair. "Do I look stupid to you? I saw the two of you together as I walked in. I saw the way she looked at you, and I also saw her kiss you."

"Sebastian it's not me, okay."

"Then who is it?"

Anton couldn't answer. He sat awkwardly holding Sebastian's stare for a brief moment before finally he looked away.

"Just as I thought."

"Look Sebastian, I think it's best if you talk to Tanya yourself," Anton sighed. "Whatever happened between you and her is really none of my business."

"That's where I think you're wrong," Sebastian said coldly. "Some friend you turned out to be Anton."

"You know what?" Anton said as he got to his feet. "I've put up with your mood swings and irrational monologues for far too long now, but I don't have to put up with this. I've got better things to do with my time."

"Fine, if that's the way it's going to be."

"Oh, and another thing," Anton said as he faced the author one last time. "I wish you did move to Alaska. Maybe being alone in some rundown log cabin in the middle of nowhere is what you really need. At least there won't be any friends around to further complicate your life."

With that said, Anton turned and walked out of the café.

10.10am

What's taking so long?

Johnno wondered what was taking Anton so long. Wasn't he just meeting the writer guy during his coffee break? Johnno had only met the man once before, but that was enough to know that he didn't really like him. The guy gave him the impression that he thought he was better than everyone else simply because he had written a book. Big deal, Johnno thought. He could write a book too if he really wanted, but as he didn't like reading in the first place where would be the fun in that?

It was already after ten o'clock. Surely the two would be finished their Wednesday morning writer's club tea party by now. He might as well save some time and walk back to the café to meet Anton. Then he would be free to spend the rest of the morning with his best friend wishing for anything they wanted. It was time to test the power of the letter they had found in the bottle. What was it really capable of delivering before sunset? Was Anton right in deciding that everything had to first come from somewhere and not simply appear out of thin air? The possibilities it seemed were endless, but as he had learnt this morning so were the consequences. They would have to think everything through carefully before they even opened their mouths.

The surf was still thumping loudly against the shore as

Johnno made his way back to Mermaids. It was a little smaller than the pair had paddled out into this morning but still a decent size by any stretch of the imagination. Perhaps before the day was out they would get the chance to go surfing together again. Right now he had to get his friend and try to see if there was some kind of way they could undo the events of this morning. Otherwise when they returned the bottle to the sea at sunset as the letter had instructed, he'd find himself waking up tomorrow morning without a job.

Johnno weaved through the tables scattered under the shade of the pandanus trees in front of the café, and stepped into the spacious, air-conditioned interior. There was no sign of Anton anywhere. Instead his eyes locked on the sight of Tanya sitting at one of the upper level tables with another man. Surely the man wearing a long sleeved business shirt on such a hot day had to be the writer guy that Anton was meeting with. Only where was Anton?

"There you are," Kim said as she suddenly appeared at his side and grabbed his arm. "I was beginning to wonder where you had gone."

The introduction obviously caught the attention of Tanya. Her eyes now locked firmly on his, to the point where the man in the business shirt turned around to see what had, or more likely *who* had distracted her from their own conversation.

"I'm sorry I left so suddenly. I had to go and find Anton," Johnno apologized.

"That's alright John," she said as she led him to one of the vacant tables beside the front counter. Away from Tanya's prying eyes. "You just sit right here and I'll go and get you that iced tea you wanted before."

Without arguing, Johnno followed her to the table and sat obediently when she pulled out the chair. He had never been to the café at this time of day before and was surprised to find that it had a more laid back feel compared to early in the morning

123

when it was a hive of activity. He hadn't sat for long before Kim returned, pulled out a chair opposite him and sat herself down with two tall glasses of iced-tea.

"How are you feeling now?" She asked while stretching her arm across the table and gently placing her hand on his. "It sounds like you've had an absolutely terrible morning."

"Yeah you could say that again," he said as he took a sip of drink. "Thanks for the drink by the way."

"Don't mention it," she smiled warmly. "So tell me, do you think it is because of the letter you found this morning?"

"I'm absolutely sure it is," Johnno answered. "I talked it over with Anton not long ago and we both think that the letter itself doesn't make your wish come true, but somehow provides the means necessary for whatever you wish for to happen."

"I'm afraid I don't understand," she said. "You wished for that rent-a-loo to fall on your bosses head and it happened right?"

"No, I didn't wish for that at all," Johnno sounded shocked by the thought. "All I wished was that something would fall from the sky and land on him. I didn't mean for a portable toilet to fall from the sky."

"But it happened didn't it," she said, more as a statement rather than a question.

"I know, in some strange kind of way that's exactly what happened. So do you see what I'm saying?"

"Not really," she shook her head. "What about the Prada handbag you wished for me? You must have said it a dozen times and the only one we saw was over the shoulder of that rich lady in the Mercedes-Benz that was here this morning. I don't think that really counts."

"But we don't know when the handbag will appear do we? No-one specified a time that it had to be here by. For all we know a courier could be delivering one to us right now."

"So you're saying the Fed-Ex man is going to deliver a Prada handbag to me today?" She asked eagerly.

124

"Maybe, but I don't exactly know," Johnno grew more confused by the minute. "What I do know is that I have to be careful what I wish for."

"Excuse me, but do you work here?" A voice suddenly interrupted them.

They both looked up to see a middle-age woman wrapped in a sarong and wearing a large brown sunhat. Underneath her hair was still wet, obviously from taking a swim in the ocean.

"Yes that's right," Kim spoke up. "I'm one of the waitresses here."

"Well sorry to interrupt you on your break," the lady continued, "but I was just walking by when I noticed that someone had obviously left their handbag behind. I thought I should hand it to someone who works here in case they come back looking for it later."

"Oh, thank you," Kim sounded surprised as the lady handed her a plain white handbag. "I'll keep it behind the counter for when they come back."

"That's alright," the lady smiled. "I just wanted to make sure it found its way into a safe pair of hands."

Kim inspected the handbag closely after the lady was gone. The element of surprise soon gave way to astonishment however. It wasn't just a handbag. It was Prada.

"Take a look at this!" Kim exclaimed. "John, it's a Prada handbag. Just like you wished for."

The lady had by now turned and left the scene, leaving only Kim and Johnno to ponder the enormity of the moment. Before they had a chance to open their mouths however there was someone else beside them at the table. Only this time it was Tanya.

"I'm sorry to interrupt the two of you. But shouldn't you be working?" She said accusingly to Kim.

"Well I was just taking my break," Kim snapped back at her. "Besides, haven't you been talking to your boyfriend for the last half hour?"

"He's not my boyfriend," Tanya answered, at the same time shooting a quick, embarrassed look in Johnno's direction. "Look all I want is a quick moment alone to talk to Johnno. It's about Anton. I promise that's all."

Kim looked uncomfortable from where Johnno sat. Reluctantly she stood to her feet still holding the handbag.

"Okay. I'll leave you alone to say whatever it is you feel you must say to him," she said. "In the meanwhile perhaps you could tell me where I can put this handbag that someone just found."

Tanya's face went blank as she stared at the handbag in Kim's hand.

"That wouldn't be a Prada handbag by chance would it?"

"As a matter of fact it is," Kim said defiantly. "It seems the letter that John found this morning is magic after all."

"But it can't be," Tanya tried to reason. Only her thoughts were all at once a tangled mess of refusing to believe and wanting to believe that her letter had taken on a power of its own. "That makes two this morning. Anton found a Prada handbag someone had left under the table only an hour earlier."

Tanya wanted this all to be a coincidence. There was no way the poem she wrote last night could have transformed itself into anything this extraordinary and magical. God wouldn't allow such a thing to happen would he? If so, had Johnno simply made a wish for someone beautiful to fall in love with him? That would explain the sudden attraction Kim had developed towards him this morning. It would also mean that there was still a chance for her to find a way of telling Johnno how she really felt about him. She only had to get Kim out of the way to do so.

"Well where do you want me to put it?" Kim asked again impatiently.

"Just leave it behind the front counter. You'll see where I've put the other one," Tanya answered quickly. She wanted her to go away so that she could talk to Johnno alone.

"So what did you want to tell me about Anton?" Johnno asked the moment Kim had left the table.

Tanya turned to face him but didn't know where to begin. She smiled as best she could, took a deep breath and mustered up the courage to finally say how she really felt about him.

"I said something to Anton this morning that may have upset him a little," she began bravely, "and I've probably just broken Sebastian's heart as well, so here goes. Johnno I know I've been mean to you in the past, but I realize now that it was only an inbuilt defense mechanism for how I really feel about you. I know you and Kim seem to have hit it off really well, but I can't stand by and watch the two of you any longer without telling you that I like you. I really like you. In fact I think I could be in love with you."

Johnno looked at her strangely. Had Tanya really just said she was in love with him? He couldn't believe that the girl who always made him feel stupid, the one who was always ready to snap at every little thing he said wrong was standing in front of him and saying she was in love with him.

"Um, Johnno," she said quietly, once more getting his attention. "When a girl says she loves you it is normally the custom for the guy to say something in return."

"I'm sorry. You've just taken me by surprise that's all," Johnno sighed. "I mean, wow. Why haven't you told me this before? I've only just met Kim and now you tell me this."

"I know, but seeing the two of you together has made me realize that it's me that should be with you, not her."

Johnno looked at her innocent face once more and could tell that she was being sincere. Only something else surged forward from the back of his mind and suddenly he could think clearly once more. Taking a deep breath he said what he thought Tanya needed to hear.

"Tanya it's not you, it's me," he began. "Can't you see? It's the letter. The only reason you are telling me this is because this morning I made a wish for you to like me. Besides, there's no guarantee that you'll still feel this way after we return the bottle to the sea at sunset."

1040am

Still looking for work

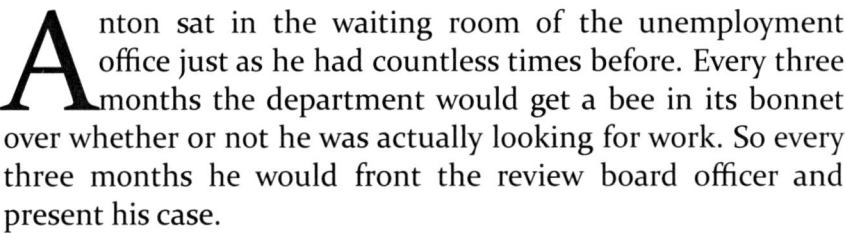

Anton sat in the waiting room of the unemployment office just as he had countless times before. Every three months the department would get a bee in its bonnet over whether or not he was actually looking for work. So every three months he would front the review board officer and present his case.

Sometimes it would simply be a matter of presenting the diary he kept of all the positions he had applied for, complete with any accompanying rejection letters advising him that he had been unsuccessful in his application. Most times that would be enough to satisfy the concerns of the disinterested worker behind the desk who was conducting the review. Only today he was asked to take a seat again as they would like to interview him in front of a panel.

The thought of being in front of a panel frightened him a little. Was this a new procedure the department had implemented? Should he have worn something more appropriate than a t-shirt and board shorts? He looked down at his feet. Perhaps flip-flops weren't the best choice of footwear either.

"Anton Rubinski?" A voice called out from across the room.

Anton stood to his feet, looked anxiously in the direction of the sizably large dark-skinned woman standing in the doorway of one of the many rooms that opened into the large waiting area and swallowed. He never liked the sound of his own surname. It only reminded him of past trips to the doctors, dentists and even the headmaster's office back when he had been at school. It seemed that anytime someone called him by his surname it had usually been preceded by an extended period of waiting uncomfortably in some clinical void of space that he'd rather not be in.

Anton walked casually towards the waiting woman, listening only to the flip-flop sound beneath his feet that now filled the room. The woman glanced disapprovingly in his direction and held the door open for him as she motioned him into the room. Anton stepped inside and looked uncomfortably at the three men in suits and ties already seated around an oval shaped table. The door clicked loudly as it closed behind him.

"Please come in Mr...Umm, I'm sorry. How exactly do you pronounce your surname?" A man with a shortly trimmed gray beard and matching gray hair spoke suddenly, peering from over the top of a silver framed pair of spectacles.

"Rubinski, as in roo-bin-ski," Anton pronounced it politely for the bearded, be-spectacled man. "It's Polish. Actually, my grandfather was Polish, my grandmother however was French. They emigrated here after they married."

"I see, well thank you," he continued, not caring for the short, family history lesson offered by the scruffy young man that had entered the room. "Mr Rubinski, please take a seat and we'll get this meeting underway."

The two other men sat silently, pens poised over the pages lined neatly on the desk in front of them. The large, dark-skinned woman now joined the three already seated at the table and motioned for Anton to sit also. Reluctantly Anton pulled out a chair at the head of the table and sat down, clutching his backpack tightly in his lap.

"So Mr Rubinski, do you understand the purpose for this meeting?" The same bearded man spoke once more.

"Umm, I think so," Anton stammered.

"It's a routine requirement of the department to review all long-term cases of those claiming unemployment benefits," the woman spoke up. Anton thought she sounded a little more consoling than the bearded fellow he seemed to have taken an immediate disliking to. "I'm sure you'll understand that it's in your best interests that we must ask you some questions."

"Yeah, sure," Anton relaxed a little and placed his backpack on the floor beside his chair.

"Mr Rubinski, exactly how long have you been out of work for?" The bearded, bespectacled man asked.

"Pretty much since I left high school," Anton answered, noticing the sudden reaction from the two other men who began to write notes in the folders in front of them.

"I see," the bearded man continued, "and in that time have you ever been in a position of employment of any kind?"

"Yes."

"In what capacity were you employed in?"

"Umm, would you mind defining exactly what you mean by capacity?"

"I beg your pardon?" The man looked questioningly in his direction.

"You said capacity," Anton corrected him. "You know - the ability to contain, absorb or hold something. Now by that do you mean a talent capable of holding a position on its own merit, or purely the capacity to be able to perform the ability or skill required to complete the task at hand?"

"Please answer the question," the man stared solemnly from the other end of the table. "Have you ever been *capable* of *holding* a position of gainful employment?"

"Yes I have." Anton held the man's stare for a moment before deciding he wasn't making the situation any better for himself by getting the man hot under the collar.

"I still don't think that answers my question," the man

131

scratched at his beard in obvious confusion. "Let me put it this way. What would you say was the greatest length of time you held a position of employment for?"

"A day," Anton answered confidently. "Let's just say that on both occasions there were professional differences which didn't lead to my being invited to return to work the next day."

"I see," he said as he glanced across at the two other men who were busy scrawling notes in their folders. "Yet obviously you come across as a very intelligent person."

"Thank you," Anton smiled casually at the reviewer.

"I don't think I intended it as a compliment," he slouched back in his chair growing frustrated by the answers he was receiving from scruffy haired upstart sitting at the end of the table.

"I'm afraid the department has been reviewing your case for quite some time now," the sizably large woman tried to add kindly. "And it is our view that you are not intent on genuinely seeking gainful employment."

"See for yourself," Anton said as he reached under the table. He unzipped his backpack and proceeded to drop the large diary he kept on the table for all to see. "The proof is all here in the diary. I've kept a record of every job I have applied for, every rejection letter I have received, dates, times, interviews."

"Mr Rubinski," the bearded man cut him short, "the department also keeps its own records. Why do you think your case was referred to me? I've personally followed up some of the job applications you have reported on the fortnightly forms that you hand in, and it is my conclusion that you had no intention of ever filling any of these positions. For that matter I have no idea how on earth you expected any of these companies to employ you based on the quality of the applications you submitted."

"What do you mean you've followed up some of my applications?" Anton asked, suddenly worried by the sight of the four review panel members gently shaking their heads in disapproval.

"We've kept a file on you for the past six weeks," the bearded man continued. "Verifying each position with every firm that you listed on your fortnightly job search reports that we require you to hand in. The results were... How can we say this? Interesting."

"Well as you can see, I'm still looking for work." Anton pushed the diary forward. Only no-one moved to pick it up.

One of the men who chose to remain quiet then handed the bearded man a folder which he duly opened and proceeded to read from a printed list that was clipped inside.

"Some of the positions you have applied for during the past six weeks include; a hotel manager, a commercial airline pilot, a deep sea fisherman, an editor for a major newspaper, the programming manager for a TV network, and my own personal favorite the IT sales director's position. Do I need to say more?"

"Mr Rubinski," the woman spoke gently to him. "How did you expect to be able to fill any of these positions?"

"Well, I was looking outside the box," he struggled to find something to say, anything for that matter that would appear to work in his favor. "I was only showing some initiative in trying to find work, that's all. I've been out of work for such a long time."

"I see," the bearded man said. Another man who had also remained silent the entire time passed a second folder to him. He opened it and began to read some of the more interesting job applications Anton had remembered writing.

"I'm writing to you to apply for the hotel manager's position. I have some wonderful ideas to improve your clientele as I have noticed there are no clothing optional resorts in your area," he read before returning the facsimiled copy of Anton's application letter to the folder and picking up the next one.

"Dear flying man, I'd love to have a chance to fly one of your planes. My favorite movie of all-time is Flying High," he paused to stare solemnly at Anton from over the rim of his glasses and then continued with the next letter anyway.

"Ahoy there captain, I'd like to apply for the deep sea fisherman's position on your pirate ship. How deep into the sea do you go? I've never been in water any deeper than waist height as I can't swim. I also get sea-sick and hate the smell of fish. But can you tell me if there is any chance of finding treasure?"

Anton noticed a smirk on the face of one of the other men sitting quietly at the table, but sensed the bearded man was only getting warmed up.

"Dear editor, I'm sorry you are getting fired. But before you go can I kindly have your job? I think I would do a much better job than you. I can't help but notice that all you ever print is bad news. Perhaps if you printed some more good news for a change then people would start buying your paper again. My neighbor's cat recently had kittens and I think that would be a more fitting headline to read from the bottom of her kitty-litter tray."

The two other men were by now doing their best not to break into a fit of laughter. Anton however sat stone faced at the end of the table, knowing that as humorous as his letters sounded there would be no laughter coming from his own mouth when this meeting was over.

"To the direct attention of the person interviewing for the network TV programming manager's position, your programming stinks! I know this isn't what you expected on a job application, but I wanted to say it just the same."

"And then there is this wonderful example which you sent for an IT sales director's position. To the IT manager, I noticed your position called for someone experienced in IT, capable of selling IT and directing a team of IT specialists in the field of IT. In asking me to take my IT skills and pursue new clients in the IT sector, I just need to know one thing. What is IT you are talking about?"

Finally he took off his glasses, returned the last of the letters to the folder in front of him and rubbed his brow in bewilderment. Beside him the two men finally let a chuckle escape, much to the disapproval of the sizable lady still seated at the table.

"Mr Rubinski," she said in total disbelief of what she had just heard. "I have to presume that you know that IT is short for information technology. So I have to ask, how on earth did you expect to be called in for an interview with job applications that were just plain terrible?"

"I guess I, uh thought..." Anton suddenly felt embarrassed in her presence.

"No, you've had more than enough opportunity to speak," the bearded man said as he put his spectacles back on. "It gives me nothing but pleasure to advise you that as of now your unemployment entitlements have formally ceased. There will be a three month period before you can officially apply for them again during which time you will still need to have shown that you were actively seeking employment. Do I make that clear enough for you?"

"Three months?" Anton exclaimed. "What am I going to do in the meanwhile? I can't survive for three months without any money. I'll get evicted from the trailer park."

"I'm sorry but the decision of the review panel is final," the woman said matter-of-factly. Anton realized now that any sympathy she may have felt for his case had disappeared the moment his applications had been read aloud.

"Look, I wish I could find a job. I really do," Anton pleaded with those gathered around the table but to no avail.

They all took turns in looking away as he looked desperately from one person to the next. All except for the gray bearded, bespectacled man who sat at the opposite end of the table.

"You want my advice?" He asked as he closed the folder in front of him. "If you put as much effort into looking for work as you did in trying to avoid it, we wouldn't be having this conversation. Get a job Mr Rubinski."

11.30am

Wish what you want

"What is taking your friend so long?" Kim asked as she marched over to where Johnno stood waiting in the shade of the tree outside the café.

"I don't know." Johnno looked around without success for any sign of his friend. "He said he was meeting with that writer guy here at the café, but when I stopped by over an hour ago there was no sign of him."

"You mean Sebastian?" Kim purred the words softly. "I heard that Tanya went on a date with him last night."

"Yeah, well that didn't stop Tanya from telling me that she is in love with me before," Johnno sighed.

"She said what?" Kim put her hands on her hips and threw a fierce look over her shoulder in the direction of the café. "I should march back inside and tell her to back off!"

"No don't do that." Johnno tried to calm her. "It's only because of the letter. After she'd been her usual mean self while I was ordering breakfast this morning, I made a wish that she would like me. I meant it only as a friend. Because she is such good friends with Anton it makes sense for the two of us to try and get along as well."

"Ah John you are such a nice man." Kim took his arm and began to lead him away from the café. "I can see now why any girl would want to make you her own."

"It just seems too weird to be anything other than the letter," Johnno continued. "She's done nothing but put me down ever since I have known her. Then suddenly I hear from her own mouth that she loves me."

"Ah that's silly." Kim held his hand tightly. "If she liked you even an ounce as much as I do, then she would have fallen in love with you a long time ago."

Johnno let her words float gently into the farthest recess of his brain. He couldn't remember a woman ever saying words that even remotely resembled what she had just said. The thought caused the corner of his mouth to crack into a smile. Her hand felt tiny and soft in his rough and manly grip, and he could sense that life was about to sail John Clark into new and unchartered waters.

"Yeah you're right Kim," he finally found the courage to say something in reply. "I'm sure everything will go back to the way it was when we throw the bottle back into the sea at sunset."

"So what do you want to do now?" Kim asked as they followed the sidewalk along the top of the beach. "Tanya made me take my lunch break now before the midday rush begins, so we have the next half hour all to ourselves."

"Well I really should find Anton to work out what we should do next with this letter," he pondered seriously for a moment. "I think we all know after the handbag incident that whatever we wish for is somehow going to happen when we least expect it."

"Like the accident at your job this morning."

"That's exactly what I'm getting at. I still can't believe I've lost my job."

"I'm sure you'll find another one," she said quickly. "Anyway, why don't you just wish for a million dollars? Then you wouldn't have to go to work and you could spend all day with me."

"I can't just wish for a million dollars," he blurted out, amused by the lack of thought she had given the matter.

"Why not?"

"For starters where is it going to come from?" He asked.

"The same place all money comes from," she said innocently, "the bank."

"Well I can't just walk into a bank and withdraw a million dollars now can I? Not unless I pointed a gun and shouted freeze."

"Oh John you are being way too serious," she laughed. "All you have to say is I wish for a million dollars and see what happens. It's just a little fun, that's all."

"No, I'm not going to say I wish for a million dollars. And I'll tell you why. It's because..."

"Ah, too late John you just said it," she laughed at him.

"See, this is what I was talking about," Johnno groaned as he realized the error he had just made. "We don't know what chain of events we've just set in motion."

"Hopefully one that will deliver a lot of money," Kim laughed again.

"I really need to find Anton so I can work out what to do next." Johnno was already feeling more than a little worried about what he had just wished for.

"Ah, don't worry about it." Kim squeezed his hand tightly. "Wish for whatever you want. Besides, I don't see Anton here. He obviously isn't interested enough to be here with his friend. Plus I have to be back at work in less than half an hour."

"Okay," he agreed reluctantly. "But only if we both promise not to change the history of the world or anything."

"Agreed," Kim nodded her head. "Now let's have a little fun."

"Well, what do you want to do first?" Johnno asked her. "Are you hungry? Would you like to go some place for lunch?"

"No, the day already feels too hot to eat," she shrugged.

"A drink then?"

"Yeah, maybe a little later though," she said as they reached the small parking lot which for much of the day was a merry-go-round of motorists looking for a space.

"What about an ice-cream?" He asked once more.

"Oh yeah," she became excited. "That's it. I wish we could have an ice-cream."

"Alright, let's head back to the café and I'll buy you one." Johnno seemed pleased by the thought of escaping the midday heat which had become stifling.

"No," she corrected him. "I wish an ice-cream man would suddenly appear and we would each get an ice-cream for free."

"I can't make a wish for that," Johnno said as he looked at her in disbelief.

"Why not?" She stared at him defiantly. "It's no different to the Prada handbag or the sausages and scrambled eggs you wished for this morning."

"I guess not," He agreed.

Only before he could make the wish he heard the not so distant sound. Feint at first, but as the van pulled into the street there was no mistaking the tune being played by the brightly painted pink and blue ice-cream van. They both watched as the ice-cream van reached the parking lot overlooking the beach and pulled up in front of them.

With mouths wide open, the two stood on the sidewalk and watched as the elderly man in the white paper hat made his way from the front of the van and stuck his head out of the side window.

"Hey would you kids like some ice-cream for free?" He asked kindly. "The generator on the ice-cream machine has just broken down and I'm going to lose the lot. I'd rather give it all away then see it go to waste."

"Yeah sure, I mean that's too bad," Johnno struggled with the words.

"We're very sorry to hear about your generator," Kim said politely, "but yes we'd love some ice-cream."

"That's good," he smiled warmly. "I'll start them coming if you can stop as many passers-by as you can."

Johnno was only more than happy to oblige and turned to a small group of walkers who were approaching. "Hey, free ice-cream. The machine is broken and he's got to give it all away."

Within minutes there was a crowd at least twenty deep at the side counter of the ice-cream van. Kim and Johnno stepped back happily and began licking the ice-cream that was melting fast in the glaring sun.

"You know what this means don't you?" Kim asked while trying to daintily wipe at a trail of ice-cream that was running down her chin.

"Of course I know what it means," Johnno replied. "My wish came true."

"No you didn't get the chance to make the wish John," she said while looking at him mischievously. "I made the wish remember? That means it was my wish that came true. Somehow I also have the power to make a wish."

"But how?" Johnno asked. "It was Anton and I who found the bottle. Not you."

"That may be true, but I was the one who opened the bottle this morning."

Johnno stopped to think for a moment if there was any way that she could be right. Had the power to make a wish been granted to her also for simply being the one to pull the cork from the bottle? What would Anton have to say about all of this?

He looked across at Kim whose thoughts were already a million miles away. It was too late. Pandora's Box had just been opened.

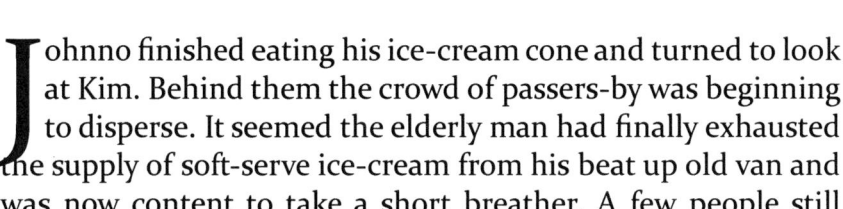

11.50am

You're a Real Hero

Johnno finished eating his ice-cream cone and turned to look at Kim. Behind them the crowd of passers-by was beginning to disperse. It seemed the elderly man had finally exhausted the supply of soft-serve ice-cream from his beat up old van and was now content to take a short breather. A few people still lingered to admire the view over the ocean.

"We have to think carefully about what we do next," Johnno said.

"Yeah, like that's ever going to happen," Kim snapped at him sarcastically. "What you're forgetting John is that I can now wish for whatever I like."

"But whatever we wish for could ultimately affect an innocent person, like the ice-cream man," Johnno said quietly as he pointed in the direction of the old man who was now slowly wiping the counter of his van.

"Ah, he'll get over it," Kim brushed aside any thought of concern.

"I need to sit down and work this out," Johnno said as he made for a nearby bench perched high above the beach.

"What's there to work out?" Kim asked. "You wish, and some way or another you get."

"But don't you realize that poor old guy has just lost his entire day's work? Not to mention the cost of repairing the generator, and who knows how much that will cost?"

"All I hear is blah, blah, blah," she mocked him. "For two people who have the power to wish for whatever they want, you and Anton have wasted half the day wishing for scrambled eggs and ice-cream. Although not together, that would just be gross."

"Actually you wished for the ice-cream," Johnno corrected her.

"Ah, you know what I mean," she sighed.

Johnno walked around to the front of the bench and sat down, half expecting Kim to sit by his side. Only when he looked to his left all he saw was a rather plain black and white handbag with some brass trinkets dangling from the strap that someone had obviously left behind. Surprised at the sight of a handbag left unattended on a park bench he reached across to pick it up. Only before his hands could reach the bag Kim had lunged across the bench from behind him and snatched it.

"Is that Prada?" She exclaimed.

"How would I know?" Johnno scoffed as he stood to face her.

"Ah, it's just a cheap handbag," she answered her own question dejectedly. "It probably cost less than ten dollars."

"But surely it has to belong to someone."

"Who cares?" She scoffed. "It's not Prada. It's not what we wished for."

Behind her Johnno could see the old man slide back behind the wheel of his ice-cream van. A part of him wanted to run over and at least pay him some money for their part in his unfortunate turn of events. It seemed the only reward he had received in return was the sight of the happy faces crammed in around the counter of his ice-cream van. He watched him drive off with a touch of sadness.

"Well actually," Johnno began, "I'm not sure what I wished for this morning while I was busy embarrassing myself and trying to figure out exactly what to say. So I made quite a few wishes for handbags. Some black, some Prada and some perhaps with dangly trinkets."

"That's right, I think I remember," she said thoughtfully. "So this was probably one of the handbags you wished for, only you didn't say Prada and all I got was a cheapie. This means that any moment now the million dollars you wished for may appear. Oh wait, I think I also may have made a wish for a million dollars. Does this mean we will get two million?"

"I don't know Kim," Johnno stopped her. "But will you listen to yourself? My former boss is in hospital at the moment because of something I wished for. So what do you think will happen for you to somehow come into possession of a million dollars?"

"I don't know," Kim snapped at him once more. "But I wish my money would hurry up and get here!"

Johnno stopped to reflect on the change that had come over her. From the moment she had discovered the letter also had the ability to grant her own wishes, a mean selfish personality had sprung up literally from nowhere. What he now saw was a side to the once likable and very pretty Asian waitress that quite plainly he didn't care much for at all.

The sound of a car backfiring suddenly turned Johnno's attention to the road that climbed uphill away from parking lot. He looked and saw that it came from the ice-cream van that had been struggling to grind its way to the top of the hill in first gear. It had come to a complete stand-still near the top of the hill with black smoke billowing out from underneath the beat up old van. Then much to Johnno's horror it began to roll backwards, slowly at first but it quickly began careering out of control.

It was surprising how much speed a rolling vehicle could gather on such a relatively short hill. Yet even more amazing was the fact that the brightly painted ice-cream van was able to achieve such a speed while traveling backwards in a perfectly straight line on its frightening descent. Johnno looked to the bottom of the hill. There was a delivery van slowly approaching the parking lot. Only it was no ordinary delivery van. It was an armored vehicle. The driver was most likely seeking only a parking space by the ocean in which to enjoy a short lunch break before delivering his load of cash to the nearest bank or countless ATM machines about town.

Kim only had time to turn around and witness the huge impact of the pink and blue ice-cream van as it slammed rear first into the back of the armored vehicle. The collision sent the armored van hurtling forward, leaping the kerb and bouncing across the sidewalk before disappearing over the edge of a ten foot rock wall. It came to a rest buried nose first in the sand with the back doors ripped wide open. On cue the beat up ice-cream van dropped over the rock wall behind it, the terrified old man still gripping the steering wheel for dear life. Once more it slammed into the back of the armored van, this time completely flipping the vehicle onto its roof.

Terrified onlookers raced to the scene, looking down in amazement at the sight of the two destroyed vehicles that lay on the beach. Luckily no-one had been sunbaking in front of the rock wall or surely they would have been killed. Johnno scrambled down the rock wall at the first sight of the old man moving inside the ice-cream van. He had been fortunate enough to survive. He only hoped he could say the same for the occupants of the armored van that lay upside down on the sand.

The next few minutes seemed a blur of people rushing past him as he tried to help the old man climb free of the wreckage. He had a cut on his forehead and appeared to be struggling to climb out of the destroyed vehicle.

"Somebody help me!" Johnno shouted over his shoulder. He struggled to take the weight of the injured man while balancing on one of the uneven shaped boulders that made up the rock wall. "I've got an injured man here."

Nobody came to his aid. Because as Johnno now saw, a gust of wind had picked up from offshore and was now blowing the contents of the armored van down the length of the beach. He stood and watched in disgust as delighted onlookers rushed past the scene of the accident, ignoring his plea for help. In their own selfish pursuit of happiness they would rather leave a man to die than miss out of the chance to grab as many hundred dollar bills as they could stuff in their pockets.

Johnno heaved the old man up and over his shoulder before carefully placing the man down on the soft sand a short distance away from the wreckage.

"Stay here," he ordered the man, realizing that even by choice the old guy didn't have any means of leaving.

He raced over to the driver's side door of the armored van and tried to open it. The door wouldn't budge. He rapped on the window and tried to peer in through the dark tinted glass, but all he could make out were the vague shapes of two occupants. He rapped furiously again on the glass and this time he thought he saw movement. Once more he banged his fist hard against the glass and this time he heard the creaking of twisted metal as the door partly opened. Johnno wrapped his fingers around the edge of the door and pulled with all his might. The door groaned and resisted stubbornly before finally opening. Johnno reached inside and grabbed the nearest man by the sleeve of his shirt. With some co-operation he was able to pull the man free. The stocky bald guy appeared relatively unscathed as he stumbled to his feet. Without hesitating, Johnno climbed back into the upside down cabin of the armored van and reached for the seatbelt that was still holding the driver in his seat. He positioned himself underneath the frame of the wiry man of Hispanic appearance and was thankful that it wasn't the stocky bald guy who had been driving.

"I hope this doesn't hurt." He said aloud as he pressed the release button on the man's seatbelt.

The man fell from his seat with a thud, and Johnno did his best to catch him. He groaned slightly as Johnno shifted the man's weight in his arms. That was good he thought. It was a sign that he was still alive. In only a few seconds Johnno had dragged him out onto the sand and over to where the ice-cream van driver still sat alone and shaken.

"What is wrong with you people?" Johnno shouted, more for his own benefit as nobody appeared interested in anything more than the impromptu money grab that was occurring along the beach. "Somebody call an ambulance."

Suddenly a gunshot rang out through the air and in that briefest of moments order was restored to Kings Beach.

When Johnno opened his eyes he saw the stocky bald man standing guard at the back of the armored van. Hand raised defiantly in the air and a wisp of smoke still trailing from the barrel of his gun. The silence that followed was deafening. All along the beach startled onlookers stood motionless with fists full of money. Their eyes trained squarely on the security guard standing vigil at the back of the armored van.

"All right," he tried his best to shout above the noise of the surf crashing against the shore. "I want everyone to return the money to the van now. Stealing from the scene of an accident is a criminal act. The serial numbers on the money are all traceable and you will be dealt with when the law catches up with you."

Those nearest to the van looked at each other, and then at the stocky bald guy with the gun. One by one they decided it would be best to co-operate, rather than take their chances at getting shot if they tried to flee the scene.

"Where am I?" The driver of the van groaned from his position on the sand beside Johnno and tried to sit up.

"Hey, take it easy buddy." Johnno gently laid him back down on the sand. "You've been in an accident. Everyone is alive but just lay still until the paramedics get here to check you out."

Satisfied by the sight of people now slowly making their way towards the van, the security guard then hurried over to where his work buddy lay resting on the sand. Behind him hundreds of beachgoers took the opportunity to hurry up the beach. Fleeing with whatever money they were holding, had stuffed down their board shorts, their bikinis or had wrapped up in their beach towels.

"Is he alright?" The security guard asked Johnno who was still waiting with the two injured drivers.

"I think so," Johnno replied. "But we need to call an ambulance for the ice-cream man. I think he's hurt bad."

"That's okay. I've already radioed police using the two-way in the van only a moment before you pulled me out. They're on their way as we speak. What on earth happened back there?"

"The engine blew up on my ice-cream van," the old man spoke up. "I'm so sorry. It started rolling backwards from the top of the hill and I didn't have any brakes."

"Hey, it wasn't your fault," the security guard said politely. "At least nobody was killed."

The sudden wail of a police siren as it raced down the hill towards the scene of the accident had every man woman and child who fancied their chances at outrunning the authorities making a last minute dash for the top of the beach. The security guard realizing that the task of stopping so many stampeding beachgoers was beyond him simply let them go. After all it was now the job of the police to secure the area from looters.

"Thanks son. You're a real hero," the security guard said as he turned to Johnno. "There should be an ambulance not far behind if you can wait with the injured drivers. I want you to stick around and give the police an eyewitness account of what happened."

With that the stocky bald guy hurried once more to the rear of the armored van and tried to reassert his authority. The two police officers were already out of their car and busy turning around disappointed beachgoers who were trying to leave the scene. Some even cried at the thought of how close they had come to leaving with thousands of dollars in cash in their arms.

Johnno watched on in disgust as they once again walked past the two injured drivers without paying them any attention. Then he noticed the familiar figure of the waitress dressed in a black t-shirt and shorts walking in the other direction. It was Kim. She was still carrying the black handbag they had found earlier, only it looked like she was...pregnant?

"Stay here," he said once more to the injured old man, again realizing that it was a stupid thing to say. "I'll be back in a second."

The two men just stared blankly in return.

"Kim," Johnno called out to her as raced across the soft sand still littered with money.

She turned at the sound of her name and caught sight of Johnno's burly frame as he plowed across the beach in her direction. The thought of being recognized only made her turn away and hurry even more determinedly to the sanctuary of the sidewalk a short distance away. It was obvious to all that her poor attempt to disguise herself as a pregnant woman holding her belly as she walked was merely a ploy to conceal what surely must amount to a lot of money hidden beneath her tight black t-shirt. Almost as surprising was the handbag that dangled from her shoulder. It was stretched to bursting point and he imagined that she must have been one of the first on the scene to start collecting as much money as she had.

"Kim, wait up," he called as he drew alongside. "What are you doing?"

"What does it look like I'm doing?" She said in frustration and finally stopped to face him once more. "I'm getting what I can and now I'm getting out of here."

"You can't keep it," he said firmly. "Now do you see why you have to be careful what you wish for? We caused this Kim, you and I together. Wishing for something like this has unleashed a chain of events that are beyond our control. You have to return the money."

148

"Why should I?" She snapped. "What's happened has happened. It's too bad it had to happen the way it did, but we can't change any of this. We can't un-wish what we've already wished for."

"Yes but it's the right thing to do."

"Well I'm not going to," she said with an air of finality. "Where has being Mr Nice guy got you in life John? You've got no job and I'll bet you didn't have the sense to pick up any money on the beach. There's enough here for both of us if you want to change your mind, but we have to go now."

"What about us?" He pleaded with her one last time. "I've still got you haven't I? Kim I'm begging you, please put the money back."

Kim looked at him longingly for a brief moment and Johnno hoped she might finally be persuaded to listen to him. Then her eyes turned cold towards him and she spoke harshly.

"I used to think you were nice. Now I only think you're a fool. I'm not listening to you, and I'm not your girlfriend."

Kim turned and hurried the short distance across the sand. She reached the small flight of stairs leading up to the sidewalk and turned to look at him one last time. Then she was gone.

12.30pm

Where did she go?

A nton walked dejectedly along the sidewalk that led away from the center of town, trying to keep to whatever shadows he could find on the steep uphill climb that lead to the beach. The temperature was still climbing and he was sure that if he listened carefully he could hear the sound of the asphalt boiling on the roadway.

He had spent the past hour wandering aimlessly up and down the main street of town. Not because he had wanted to buy anything, but purely because the shady tree lined street had offered a least some respite from the midday sun. Soon he had discovered that stepping into the occasional air-conditioned shop had the effect of cooling his sweat drenched t-shirt. After loitering for a few moments and pretending to browse, he'd step outside again and the dampness would feel cool and refreshing against his skin. There was only so long however that he could keep up the charade of window-shopping until the moment of realization arrived that he in fact had no money to spend. Then the whole process seemed pointless and futile.

Upon reaching the crest of the hill his t-shirt once more felt hot and drenched against his skin, but at least a cool breeze had picked up from off the ocean. Before him the sea stretched as far as the eye could see. It sparkled blue and inviting until it collided in the distance with a clear blue summer's sky. Hopefully by mid afternoon the breeze would be enough to cool the temperature by a few degrees. Although an onshore wind this strong would also be more than capable of reducing the surf he had enjoyed this morning to nothing more than a choppy mess of whitewater before the day was over.

The sidewalk he had followed from the main street of town seemed to twist and turn in its attempt to avoid the shadows on its long descent to the beach. Anton was sure the flip-flops beneath his feet would start melting on the hot concrete if he didn't reach Mermaids soon. Fortunately he could already see the parking lot in front of the café, so he knew it wouldn't be much longer until he would step underneath the giant blower once more and into the cool air-conditioning that was waiting for him inside. He crossed the road and as expected the tiny gravel stones on the roadway released themselves from the gooey mess of melted tar and stuck to the under sole of his flip-flops. He tried to ignore the horrible grating noise they made underneath his feet, and when he reached the opposite side of the road he began scraping the stones off on the concrete sidewalk. As he did so he looked around and was surprised to notice just how busy the café looked.

Outside, every table under the giant pandanus tree was occupied. People milled about excitedly, blocking the sidewalk that ran along the beach and the clusters of tables that also spilled out onto it. Anton shuffled politely past a small crowd of people standing in the doorway sipping their iced-teas and stepped inside. The scene was just as busy. Fortunately he caught sight of Tanya at the rear of the café clearing tables, and excused himself repeatedly as he quickly made his way through the crowd to reach her.

"Tanya," he called above the noise of excited people. "What's going on? Why are all these people here?"

"Anton," she turned around and seemed pleased to see him. "I'm glad you're here. Where's Johnno?"

"I don't know I've only just come back from my so-called meeting in town," he sighed.

"Anton I need you to find Johnno," she said firmly.

"Why? Is he in some kind of trouble?"

"How would I know?" She appeared flustered. "But if you find Johnno you'll find Kim. And then you can tell her to get back here so the owners can let her have it!"

"Kim's not here?" He seemed confused. "Where did she go?"

"She took her break over an hour ago and left with Johnno," she said as she continued to work, stacking empty cups and plates into the small tray that she held pressed into her side. "Look, I can't talk now because Kim was supposed to be back from her break half an hour ago and for some reason the place is full of cashed-up merrymakers who seem to be in a party mode. We're lucky the owners stopped in to see how things were going because there is no way the chef and I could have coped with this rush on our own."

"I wish I knew where Johnno was," Anton sighed. "But if he's with Kim then I wouldn't know where to begin looking."

"In the meantime could you do me a huge favor, as a friend?" She pleaded with him.

"Yeah sure. Just tell me what it is," he agreed without even waiting to hear what she would ask.

"Can you take over clearing the tables for me? The owners are both busy behind the front counter, the chef is swamped in the kitchen and I'm trying to clear tables and bring out orders at the same time."

"You want me to clear tables?" He looked at her in disbelief.

"There's a black apron hanging on the back of the door in the kitchen. All you have to do is collect any empty cups and plates in this tray, take them to the kitchen and stack them in the dishwasher. The chef will show you how to turn it on when it's full so that one is washing while you unload the other. Follow me and I'll show you where everything is."

"Alright, I guess," he said as he followed her to the kitchen, not really having a choice in the matter. "But I wish the place wasn't so busy."

When he emerged he was wearing a black apron and clutching the empty tray, ready to work. Tanya had disappeared with as many orders as she could carry, ready to deliver to the tables of hungry patrons that filled the café to capacity. He couldn't remember the place ever being this busy. It seemed he had picked the worst day possible to volunteer. Slowly he began to wander amongst the tables, carefully stacking cups, plates and dirty cutlery onto the large tray that Tanya had gleefully shoved into his hands. When it was full he returned to the kitchen and stacked them in the dishwasher, just as Tanya had demonstrated briefly, and returned to repeat the process once again.

On his third trip out amongst the tables, Tanya had called out to him and motioned quickly at the television that was mounted on the wall. Someone was standing on a chair trying to turn the volume up and the whole room had immediately fallen into silence.

"What is it?" He whispered as he hurried to her side.

"It's the beach right outside the café," she sighed in amazement at the wreckage that was being beamed live from the far end of Kings Beach.

Anton's jaw dropped when suddenly the cameras cut to Johnno and the burly image of his friend filled the TV screen just as the volume turned up.

"...How does it feel to be hailed a real hero in the wake of this extraordinary accident?"

"I don't know if hero is the word, I only did what I thought was the right thing to do. I'm glad no-one was seriously injured, although I feel really bad for the driver of the ice-cream van who

was taken to hospital. It was just terrible luck for his van to give up on him like that and roll backwards downhill."

"Yes a terrible turn of events and I'm told terrible scenes earlier as hundreds of beachgoers selfishly rushed past the injured and began looting the armored van as its contents blew along the length of the beach. Police have now closed the beach and are still in the process of collecting money as it washes ashore following this morning's bizarre accident. At this stage it is believed that the armored van was carrying in excess of two million dollars. Police are advising any locals that may have pocketed some of the cash to return it to the temporary desk they have set up in the parking lot. Reporting live from Kings Beach this has been..."

"Boo!" The crowd joined in unison as they jeered the female reporter on the TV and the same man who had turned up the volume now killed the sound on the TV and hopped down off the chair.

"Alright, if any of this is true then I want you all out of my café now!" A voice suddenly boomed loud enough to be heard above the noise of the crowded room.

Tanya turned around to see her boss standing red-faced in the doorway, clearly angered by what he had just heard. Over by the counter his wife had stopped serving the customers at the cash register while her husband let loose at the packed house.

"I am not going to be used to launder any more missing money and I suggest you do as the reporter said and return it to the police desk now," he said angrily. "This café is now closed."

"You can't do that," one man had the nerve to backchat the owner.

"Just watch me," he barked back in his direction. "Exactly how many wet hundred dollar bills do you think I have put through my till in the last half hour? And when I return them to the police who do you think is going to be out of pocket? Would that be you? What about the people who have worked hard to make your coffees and bring your lunches to the table? What do they get? I am not going to conduct my business using stolen money so I'm asking you all to leave."

Anton and Tanya stood silently and watched as the entire café began to slowly empty out onto the sidewalk. A few paused to linger while they stared at the now empty beach in front of them, but most chose to drive off in their cars or simply disappeared into the blistering heat of the afternoon.

Anton couldn't remember the place ever looking so deserted.

The owner now satisfied that he had wiped his hands clean of any involvement in the scandal turned and headed toward the kitchen. He only took a few steps however before he stopped and stared questioningly at the sight of Anton wearing a black apron and still clutching the tray of collected china.

"I'm terribly sorry," he said softly to the tall man with the scruffy dark blonde hair standing before him. "But who are you? Do you work here?"

"Well, umm, no," Anton said apprehensively. "I'm just a good friend of Tanya's. I could see that you were really busy so I thought I'd help out by clearing the tables for her."

"Actually I asked him to help out," Tanya said. "He's been a good friend of mine for four years, and he comes here almost every day, so he kind of already knew where everything was. I hope you didn't mind, he was only going to help me clear tables until Kim showed up."

Anton looked nervously at the medium built man with the jet black hair and smooth olive skin. He seemed to take an eternity to figure out just what to say next. Anton wondered what he must think of his scruffy appearance and the pair of flip-flops he wore on his feet. The last thing he wanted to do was get Tanya in trouble.

"Not at all, that's fine," he replied calmly to Tanya.

Anton finally let out the breath he had been holding in.

"I'm Jake," he introduced himself and stretched out his hand.

"Anton," he followed with a short reply and the two men shook hands.

"That is my wife Jenna on the register," he pointed to the lady behind the counter who politely waved in return. "We're the owners of this little café."

"Well it's very nice to meet you," Anton replied politely. "I guess I'll hang the apron back behind the door now that the rush seems to be over. I hope I haven't caused any problem."

"Don't be silly, of course you haven't," Jake replied warmly. "In fact thank you for helping out, even if it was only for a short while."

"Hey, no problem," he smiled in Tanya's direction. "What are friends for right?"

"So tell me Anton," Jake looked at him seriously for a moment, "have you had any experience working in a café before?"

"I'm afraid not," Anton smiled. "Although I do come here for breakfast most mornings, and I have tried everything on the menu at least once."

"So what are you doing for work at the moment?"

"I'm umm, still looking for work," Anton felt a little embarrassed. "Only as of today I've decided I'm going to have to try a little harder."

"Well, how would you like to start work here?" He looked thoughtfully at Anton, perhaps still deciding whether his offer was a little premature. "That is if you are interested. I can teach you everything you need to learn. The espresso machine will take a little time to master, but I could show you how to use the register and take orders. You'll still have to do a lot of the mundane chores like clearing tables and washing dishes, but I like your initiative. So what do you say?"

"Are you serious?" Anton seemed surprised by his offer.

"Only if you take your job seriously, unlike that other girl who just seemed to disappear," he said casually.

156

"Why sure. Thank you," Anton answered in amazement. "Thanks Jake, I won't let you down."

"Okay," he agreed, at the same time becoming a little distracted at the sight of the two police officers who had just entered the café. "Well if you can continue clearing tables for now, I'll come see you in a minute and we'll sit down and talk about your hours, pay, and uniform and so on."

Anton and Tanya watched as Jake walked over to the two uniformed police officers and began talking animatedly about the events that had just unfolded.

"I can't believe he just offered you a job," Tanya seemed as shocked as he was.

"I know, neither can I," Anton shook his head in disbelief.

"No, I guess it's more that I can't believe you accepted his offer. When did you change your mind about actually wanting to work for a living?"

"I guess since my meeting this morning with the unemployment office," he smiled. "They canceled by benefits. Not that it matters now I'll get to hang out with you all day."

"That's great Anton," she smiled. "As long as you realize that I don't just get to hang out. We actually do have to work during the day. In fact, as you've seen it can get quite busy at times. Today has just been nuts."

"That's it," Anton exclaimed.

"What's it?"

"Suddenly it all makes sense," he looked at Tanya excitedly. "The job offer from out of nowhere and the crowd suddenly leaving before, can't you see? It has to be the letter. At the review meeting this morning I'm sure I remember saying that I wished I could get a job, and now bingo. I have one. Then a few moments ago when you asked me to help clear the tables I said I would. Only I wished it wasn't so busy. Then suddenly the owner kicked everyone out."

"Are you sure?" She seemed annoyed at the thought. "I thought we'd all forgotten about the bottle by now."

"Oh I don't see how you could have forgotten about it," Anton looked directly at her.

"What's that supposed to mean?"

"What color nail polish are you wearing Tanya?" He smiled at her. "Is it the same color as the love heart you painted on the letter?"

"*You know it was from me?*" She went red from embarrassment. "How long have you kept this quiet?"

"I figured it out sometime before Sebastian arrived this morning," he said calmly. "But I didn't want to say anything until I was convinced beyond doubt that the whole thing wasn't purely a coincidence. Don't you understand? It works Tanya. The poem you wrote in that letter actually works."

"How can you be so sure?" She asked.

"Because I have a job," he smiled. "And I'm sure once we find out what Johnno and Kim have been up to this morning we'll know a bit more about the sudden and unexplained appearance of money on the beach."

"Well if you want to keep your job you'd better get to work," she sighed. "At least until we've had a chance to talk to Johnno."

"Okay," Anton replied as he turned to view the now empty café. "Man they sure left a mess on the tables when everyone cleared out."

He had only managed to fill the tray one more time with the empty plates before Tanya was once more at his side.

"You'll never guess what someone has left behind on a chair," she said with a hint of amusement.

Anton turned to see what she was holding in her hand. It was another handbag. A small, black crocodile skin, oversized purse with silver trinkets dangling from the zip.

"And it's Prada."

158

1.05pm

I want to sell

Sebastian opened the door and stepped into the cool interior of the tiny sales office. His entrance barely raised an eyebrow from Ben and certainly didn't justify Walter pulling his nose out of the horse racing guide he spent most of the day hiding behind. He quietly walked over to his desk and checked for any messages that may have been left while he was out to lunch. There were none.

It was always like this in the middle of the day. Most likely it would be for the next twenty years, if he decided to stick around that long just to prove the point. Sebastian stood behind his desk without feeling the need to pull his chair out and settle in for another afternoon of pretty much the same. There were decisions he reminded himself, and there were bad decisions. To not make a decision at all he thought was quite possibly the worst decision one could make. To some degree it was indecision that had kept him in this job for so long. Not knowing what to do when his career as a writer had slammed head first into a brick wall. One grew tired after so long of looking at the pieces that lay crumpled at his feet. Eventually you had to pick up the pieces and move on, or find another way over the wall.

Unfortunately his judgment had been clouded by the thought of the pretty waitress he had been infatuated with for the past year. He'd been holding a door open in the hope that there may be a chance for the two of them to create a future of their own. Oh well. You know what they say, when one door closes another door always opens. If his date last night with Tanya hadn't been enough for him to realize that door had now closed, the brief conversation with her this morning certainly had been. Initially he thought the problem may have been that she was a Christian, whereas he was happy enough to say he believed that God existed and leave it at that. Instead it was something far easier for him to understand. Sometimes as she had explained, it takes being with the wrong person to realize who the right one is that you are meant to be with. As it turned out it was Johnno that Tanya was interested in, and not Anton as Sebastian had suspected.

He felt bad for Anton. He had directed the full brunt of his frustration at him this morning. Not just for the fact that his date last night with Tanya had ended awkwardly, but for everything. The job he was stuck in, his failed writing career and even the incessant heat that was driving him mad. All morning his mind had turned over his conversation with Anton, and each time he had arrived at the same conclusion. Anton was right. It was time he made up his own mind about what he wanted to do in life. Sometimes it is easier to try and shift the blame onto other people for the decisions we are too afraid to make than admit it is our own indecisiveness that is preventing us from moving forward.

'Ooh, I like that line,' he stopped to ponder the full meaning of the words that came to mind. 'Perhaps one day I'll get the chance to use it in a book.'

Ben by now was looking curiously at Sebastian through the window of his office. Perhaps wondering why he was standing behind his desk and staring blankly into space. Finally convinced that this was what he wanted to do, Sebastian strode confidently across the room and stopped in the doorway of Ben's office.

160

"Hey, what's on your mind?" Ben asked, now surprised by how quickly Sebastian seemed to snap out of his trance-like state and suddenly appear in the doorway to his office.

"I'm just wondering how much you think my house is worth?" Sebastian asked while casually leaning against the door frame. "You know the one on top of Kings View Terrace? Four bedrooms, two bathrooms, double lock-up garage. Kind of has an ocean view if you stand on the tip of your toes and look out the bedroom window."

"Hard to say," Ben paused as he chewed the end of his pen. "Why, are you thinking of selling?"

"Yeah, as a matter-of-fact I am," Sebastian answered. "Provided I can get the right price for what I have in mind."

"Sure, I understand. Look I'm free now if you want to sit down and talk things over," Ben for once seemed genuinely keen to talk to him. "What's brought this on all of a sudden? You thinking of downsizing or are you just after a change of scenery?"

"Oh I think a change of scenery best describes it," he answered.

Sebastian tried not to see the question of downsizing as anything other than the man doing his job. A part of him took that as a sign of personal growth. Finally it seemed he wasn't interpreting everything that Ben said as a thinly veiled personal attack on his writing career. Another part of him however was still convinced that any niceness on his part was purely the result of sensing that there might be something in this for him. Whatever the real truth of the matter was, he thought he owed it to Ben and Walter to entrust them with the sale of his house.

"Okay, well what are your plans once you sell?" He asked. "Was there something in the window that caught your eye? That is if purchasing another property is what you had in mind?"

"Actually I think I may already have found something on the internet," Sebastian said coolly. "So I don't think you'll be able to help me with that side of things."

"You haven't already spoken to another agent about this other property have you Sebastian?" Ben asked with a touch of concern. "Because you know Walter and I will look after you on this one don't you? I mean all jokes aside about your writing and everything. We see more of each other at this place than we do our own families. I'd kind of like to do this one as a favor to you."

"Really?" Sebastian seemed surprised by his generous offer.

"Yeah, of course," he replied sincerely. "If I can help you out with the sale of your house then you won't have to worry about paying any agent's commission. I'll even give you a run through of the whole process if you like so you can see what is involved in selling a property from this side of the desk. Maybe then the idea of finally taking the real estate course and getting your accreditation won't seem like such a bad idea."

"Boy, I don't know what to say Ben," Sebastian wondered for a moment if perhaps he had misjudged Ben the entire time he had known him. "I guess thank you, that's very generous."

"Did I hear you say you're thinking of selling?" Walter's voice boomed from the next room. Suddenly, Sebastian could hear the sound of Walter's heavy footsteps hurrying toward him. They stopped when his huge frame filled the doorway to Ben's office. Sebastian felt that he had nowhere left to stand and so he sat himself down on one of the chairs in front of Ben's desk.

"So where is this other property you have in mind?" Ben asked as he leant back in his chair. "Is it somewhere close-by that we can go and take a look?"

"You know it's a wonderful opportunity Sebastian for you to get some experience with what is involved with selling a property," Walter continued his own conversation. "I've always said to Ben that I could picture you one day making sales. There's no reason why you still can't write books and sell houses too."

"So anyway," Ben said, returning to the topic of the other property, "what about this place you've found on the internet? Are you able to show it to me? I might still be able to make an approach on the property through the agent provided it isn't listed exclusively."

"Oh I can show you if you like," Sebastian sighed. "Only it's in Alaska."

"You're kidding me," Ben said, nearly falling off his chair at the mention of the word, "Alaska?"

"Yeah, that's right," Sebastian answered, waiting for the tirade of mockery he was sure would follow.

"Why on earth would you want to move there?" Walter looked at him dumbfounded as he stood motionless in the doorway of Ben's office. "Why would you want to leave the warmth of Kings Beach to go live in one of the coldest places on earth? You may as well go and live inside an icebox if you ask me."

"Nothing's wrong with Kings Beach," Sebastian tried to explain. "It's just that I need a change of scenery for a while. I've been thinking about this for the past year. I really want to go to Alaska, and not just for a holiday. I want to get a real feel for the place, experience a different lifestyle altogether and write my next book. I feel I owe it to myself to try one more time to write a story that I'm proud of. It doesn't have to be a bestseller. But if I'm going to look at doing something different with my life, like sitting the course and going into real estate, then I don't want to turn my back on a career as a writer on account of one book that was considered a failure."

"Hey we don't think you're a failure Sebastian," Ben spoke quietly now. "In fact, I'm really sorry if I ever made you feel that way."

"After the reviewers tore my second book to pieces, it becomes hard to avoid feeling like one," he admitted.

"To be honest I haven't read any of your books," Ben confessed. "But I've only joked around with you about your writing when you made it seem more important than your job, like you didn't need to be here because you've earned a lot of money from your books in the past. I guess I imagined that you thought you were more important than us."

"I never meant to guys," Sebastian now felt he needed to apologize to both of the men in the room. "In fact there's another reason I need to sell my house. I can't afford to stay there."

"So Alaska is the answer huh?" Ben pondered this for a moment. "Are you sure this is what you want to do?"

"Yeah, I figure I can sell up, buy a log cabin on five acres of pristine wilderness and still have over a hundred thousand in my bank account," he reasoned.

"And what will you do when you finish writing your next book?" Ben asked him.

Sebastian thought about the question for a moment. It was a good question, a fair question, and one for which he did not have an answer. He hadn't yet thought that far into the future.

"Umm, to be honest I have no idea," he confessed.

"What if you've had enough of the cold by then, will you want to come back?" Walter now asked him.

"I think it goes without saying that one day I'll come back," Sebastian replied. "I don't know when that's likely to be though. All I know is that I'll live to regret it if I don't go."

"I see." Ben's mind was already racing ahead. "And how long is it going to take exactly to write this book? You know if you didn't have to work or anything?"

"I guess about twelve months," Sebastian thought for a moment. "That gives me enough time to get a real feel of the place and also a chance to experience the change of seasons over the course of the year."

"Okay well let's take a look at this property you found online first and I'll see what background information I can dig up on it." Ben spun the monitor of his computer around to face Sebastian and adjusted the keyboard and mouse so he could use it without reaching across the desk. "If you can get it up on screen for us to see, I might just have a few suggestions you may not have thought about."

Sebastian felt a little awkward while typing in the website address and searching for the property he had looked at time and time again while the two men watched over his shoulder. When he finally slouched back in the chair and watched the two men peer inquisitively at the property description that displayed a picture of the humble cabin set against the forest, he wondered if he had perhaps lost his mind.

"Looks like a rat-infested hobble of a shack to me," Walter blurted out loud without any care for anyone else's opinion.

"Let me ask you something Sebastian," Ben said as he turned to face him. "Are you planning to go over there and write a book, or spend the year renovating a cabin in the middle of nowhere?"

"Well the whole idea is to get away from everything and clear my head so I can write," he explained.

"Is it likely to be a problem that there's no electricity, no running water and no sewage? Although there is a separate outhouse and it does say the property adjoins two freshwater streams. But the nearest town is twenty-five miles away. That's a long way to travel for take-out, unless you plan on going hunting for your food." Ben looked again at the picture and screwed up his nose before typing the lot number of the property into a database of some sort and coming up with a screen full of information that Sebastian had not seen. "Says here the property has been on the market for over two years, asking price is forty-nine thousand but it last sold for forty-five only three years ago. Can I make a suggestion here?"

"Yeah sure," Sebastian now looked at him anxiously.

"Don't make the same mistake of buying this property that the current owner did," he said matter-of-factly. "I'm sure you'll find a much nicer place to rent for twelve months that is less isolated and has your basic facilities including running water and electricity. Any maintenance will be taken care of by the landlord and you'll be free to write for the entire time in peace and quiet. Then as soon as you've had enough of the cold and want to come back to sunny Kings Beach, you won't be waiting two years for the next sucker to buy the place from you."

Sebastian could see he had a point, and a very good one at that. He hadn't even thought about how he would set his computer up without there being any electricity.

"That sounds like a much better idea if you ask me," Walter agreed with Ben. "And if this is something you feel you really must do Sebastian, then providing you're willing to finally sit the course and get your real estate accreditation, there'll be a job waiting for you when you return."

"Really?" Sebastian seemed surprised at the support now being thrown in his direction from two people he'd often thought had only longed to bring him down to earth at every opportunity.

"Of course," he replied, puzzled as to why Sebastian would at all doubt him. "I'm always telling people that I work with a writer. I kind of hope that in saying so that some of your celebrity status might rub off on me, at least in their eyes. So if this is what you feel you must do, then by all means go ahead and do it."

"Thanks Walter, that really means a lot to me," Sebastian replied. "Of course it still depends entirely on me being able to sell my house before I can even think about going to Alaska."

"I'm sure that Ben will take care of that for you. I'll leave the two of you to work out the details," Walter said before patting him on the shoulder and shuffling back to his desk.

"I've just had an idea about how I can free up some equity for you while at the same time keeping you in the property market in Kings Beach while you're gone," Ben suddenly snapped his fingers as the thought came to him.

"I can't see how I can afford to do both," Sebastian admitted. "I need the money for the trip, and I'll have no income while I'm away."

"That's right. So my idea will work perfectly," Ben said

excitedly. "I've heard that developers are ready to begin selling some luxury apartments straight off the plan for a new project that is about to get underway. We're talking a choice of two or three bedroom apartments, all with water views, a pool, tennis courts, secure entry and a reserved parking space in the basement. The beauty of it is they won't be available to move into for another twelve months. All they're asking is a five percent deposit and the apartment is secured for twelve months interest free with no repayments. By the time you've finished writing your book the apartment will be ready to move into. Surely the repayments would be much less expensive than what you're paying for your house. Heck you could put a deposit down on two apartments and sell the other for a small profit when you get back."

"That sounds great," Sebastian became excited at the thought. "Where are they going to be built?"

"We're talking absolute waterfront, right at the mouth of the river with views facing straight out to sea. Only they can't make the announcement until tomorrow," Ben explained. "The developers have just bought the Kings Beach Holiday Park and the owners are having a meeting with the park residents today to let them know when they have to be out, but the timing couldn't be more perfect. We can have a look at your house this afternoon if you like and then we're ready to be one of the first to sign when they make the announcement."

It sounded perfect Sebastian thought. Except for one small detail, the Kings Beach Holiday Park was where Anton lived.

2.00pm

Man of the Hour

Johnno was relieved to finally be able to leave the scene of the accident. The detectives had insisted it would only take a few minutes for him to answer their questions. An hour later he felt that he strongly disagreed with their concept of time. The clean up was already well underway. Teams of officials were combing the beach a second time, looking for any money they may have initially missed. A second armored van was now stationed in the parking lot and a team of security guards were busy tagging the bags of cash salvaged from the beach and loading them into the back. A large mobile crane and two flatbed trucks were parked nearby on the hill. Waiting until the beach was given the all-clear before they moved in to remove the stricken vehicles, because as Johnno had learnt during the past few hours, money was everything.

A small crowd of onlookers were still watching the scene from their vantage point on the sidewalk at the top of the sand dune. Not surprisingly, anyone who had been here when the contents of the armored van had blown along the beach like dry leaves on an autumn day had long gone. They would have been foolish to hang around and risk being approached by the police once their search had widened to include anyone with a sizable bag and a smile on their face.

Johnno rounded a small bend in the path and headed for the café. At least he was sure to have a story to tell Anton, if indeed he was there. He'd been impossible to find since their conversation on the beach this morning shortly before he had left to meet with that writer guy. Johnno still couldn't understand why meeting with someone who came across as a stuffy know-it-all was more important than spending the day with his best friend and devising a list of things they could wish for.

The umbrellas out front of the café flapped a little in the cool breeze that had picked up from off the ocean, bringing with it a pleasant drop in temperature. Clouds had begun to gather on the horizon and he now thought there was a chance of an afternoon storm developing. Maybe if he was lucky he'd still be able to hit the surf with Anton before it arrived.

Johnno however was blown away the minute he stepped inside the cool air-conditioned café and his eyes fell upon the bevy of gorgeous bikini-clad girls occupying the tables. Johnno blinked twice, convinced himself they were real and stepped outside again. Sure enough there was a small mini-bus in the parking lot outside the café. The sign in the front window of the bus read USA beach volleyball tour. He returned inside, aware now that his actions had attracted some rather curious glances from the girls. Johnno knew they were here purely because Anton had made a wish this morning for a busload of gorgeous beach volleyball players to appear, and there was no denying they all looked gorgeous.

Trying hard not to stare as he walked past their table, he instead kept his eyes open for any sign of Anton. Fortunately he spotted his friend at one of the tables on the upper level, sitting opposite a man he hadn't seen before. It looked like the two had just finished an in-depth conversation as they both stood up and shook hands before the other man disappeared into the kitchen.

"Hey aren't you the guy who was just on TV?" One of the

bikini-clad girls politely tapped his arm as he walked slowly past her table. "Oh my goodness, you are!"

Johnno turned around but didn't know what to say to the dazzling brunette with the knockout smile, especially when the entire table of volleyball players then turned to stare at him.

"Hey you're right," another girl said excitedly. "It's the guy who rescued those men on the TV report."

"Wow, you're like a hero after what you did on the beach," the brunette said as she smiled at him. "Did you get hurt when you pulled that man out of the wreck?"

"No, I'm fine actually," were the only words he could say in defiance to the butterflies that danced in his stomach.

"Why don't you come join us for a drink? Then you can tell me all about it," she said as she seductively bit her lower lip.

"Actually I, umm..."

"Hey Johnno," Anton's voice called out from across the room as he beckoned excitedly for his friend to come and join him.

Johnno turned to look at his friend and then once more at the brunette seated at the table. For the likes of him he didn't know what to do.

"Umm, perhaps I should go see what my friend wants," he said politely to the girl.

"That's alright," she continued talking sweetly to him. "Your friend is welcome to come and join us too if that's what you want."

"There you are Johnno," Tanya said as she suddenly appeared from nowhere. She then planted an affectionate kiss on his cheek before snuggling up at his side, drawing a curious look from the girl he had just been talking to. "I was wondering where the man of the hour had got to."

Johnno watched the brunette turn up her nose at the sight of Tanya. Her attention suddenly returned to her friends and in an instant it seemed that he was yesterday's news.

Tanya had watched the entire scene unfold from behind the

cash register. Fortunately she had been in the process of finishing up for the day, now that the afternoon staff had arrived to start their shift and the police had advised Jake he was free to continue trading. When Johnno had entered the café alone, she had taken that as her sign that perhaps Kim was now out of the picture and she was finally free to make a move on the man she had long fancied. Only before she had time to move from behind the counter, the brunette with the hungry eyes had stopped him dead in his tracks. Well she wasn't going to let another girl steal his attention. It was time to make her move, be bold and in the process hope that there was a way that this would all somehow work out.

Right now she had him by the arm, and was leading him away from any thoughts of bikini-clad volleyball players she was sure would only hinder him from being able to see her true feelings for him. If in fact that wasn't already too late.

"Johnno, don't even think of looking at her," she said when she caught him about to turn and look over his shoulder. "A girl like that will only break your heart."

"What was all that about?" He asked her, totally confused as to how she had managed to sweep in and usher him away. "They were..."

"Only here in the first place because Anton made a wish for them to be here," she cut him off playfully. "Anton has told me all about it."

"He has?" Johnno asked as he tried to calculate exactly how long he'd been gone.

"You on the other hand have some explaining to do," she said, still being mindful to keep her voice sounding sweet and lovely. "Like how all that money came to be on the beach and where Kim has disappeared to?"

She stopped in front of the table where Anton sat and forced Johnno's shoulders down until he had no choice but to sit also. Then she quietly slipped into the chair opposite him.

"Where have you been dude?" Anton quizzed him the second his behind touched the chair.

"Where have I been?" Johnno seemed amused by his question. "Where have you been all morning? I've been looking everywhere for you. You just disappeared after you said you were going to meet that writer guy."

"Well I had that meeting at the unemployment office."

"Oh yeah," Johnno said as he remembered just how busy his unemployed friend's day had been. "I forgot all about it. How'd that go?"

"Ah, they canceled my benefits," Anton said with a smile on his face.

"Then why are you so happy?" Johnno asked before noticing the strange black thing that was tied around his waist. "And what's with the apron?"

"That my friend is what I'll be wearing as of tomorrow when I start working here."

"Get out of here!" Johnno seemed shocked at the thought of Anton actually being excited at the thought of work. "When did this happen?"

"This morning while I was pleading with the review panel to not cancel my unemployment benefits, I may have accidently wished that I could find a job," he said proudly. "And then after half of the beachgoers suddenly became a few hundred dollars richer, I gave Tan a hand to help out and somehow that impressed Jake the owner enough that he then offered me a job."

"And you're happy about this right?" He quizzed him further.

"Yeah of course I am. I only sit around here most of the day like a fly on the wall while you all go off to work, so I may as well clear some tables and get paid to be here. It wasn't like I had any other job prospects on the horizon."

"I had no choice but to ask him," Tanya spoke up, trying her best not to vent her frustration at Johnno. "Kim failed to come back from her lunch break and all I knew was that she was with you. What happened, did the two of you break up?"

"Well I guess we did, if you could really say we were even together to begin with," he sighed. "It's a long story, but she made a wish for an ice-cream and then for a million dollars and somehow caused the whole mess on the beach."

"Wait a minute," Tanya said as she looked at him angrily. "You're telling me that Kim has the power to make a wish too?"

"Yeah I guess so," Johnno answered and shrugged his shoulders. "After all, she was the one who pulled the cork out of the bottle. The problem now is that I don't have a clue where she is, and we have no idea what she is wishing for."

"You must have some idea where she went?" Anton pressed him for information.

"The last I saw her, she yelled that I wasn't her boyfriend and waddled away looking like a pregnant woman from all the money she'd stuffed up her shirt," he said dejectedly.

"Well perhaps that will be the last you'll see of her." Tanya gently rubbed his back and felt bad for the fact that Kim had obviously hurt him, yet seized another opportunity to stick a knife in Kim's back all the same. "You don't want a woman like that in your life."

"And you're only being nice to me because I made a wish for you to like me." Johnno gently grabbed her hand to stop her repeated back rubbing.

"I am not." Tanya seemed hurt by his remark. "I thought I made it perfectly clear how I feel about you this morning."

"Can't you see it's the letter Tanya?" Johnno tried to reason with them both. "We haven't been able to figure out a way that we can use it for good without hurting someone else in the process. On top of that, Kim is out there somewhere wishing for who knows how many more handbags and the last thing we need is another disaster to fall in our laps because of it. We have to put the letter back in the bottle and throw it back into the sea to take the power away from her."

"How is that going to help?" Anton asked him.

"Because that's what I wrote at the end of the poem," Tanya answered for Johnno.

"Excuse me, but your poem?" Johnno looked at her in bewilderment. "You put the message in the bottle?"

"That's right." She let the words float across the table.

Johnno was speechless.

"It's alright dude. It took some time for me to figure out it was her too," Anton offered before thinking aloud, "there must be something we can wish for that isn't going to directly impact someone else."

"Yeah, but like what?" Johnno still seemed shocked at the thought of it being Tanya who wrote the letter. "And when we return the bottle to the sea, there's no guarantee that we'll still have whatever we wish for in our possession when the sun finally sets on this crazy day."

"Not so my friend," Anton interrupted him. "That's where we need to think outside the box. I have a job that I'm starting tomorrow, and I fail to see how that is going to hurt anyone."

"Yeah you're right." Johnno's eyes lit up once more. "Hey Tanya, if you wrote the poem then you must know how we can make a wish for something without it inflicting loss or pain on someone else."

"Look I'm sorry Johnno, but all I wanted to do was brighten up someone else's day. I didn't write any rules before I threw the bottle into the sea, and I certainly didn't want to believe that this whole thing was anything more than a coincidence. It's my birthday, that's all. I just wanted to let go of some painful memories and make a fresh start."

"There must be at least one thing that we can wish for that can make each of our lives better before we throw the bottle back into the sea," Johnno spoke up. "It's Tanya's poem, I think it's only fair that we include her in some way. But I wish I knew what we could wish for without having someone else hurt in any way."

The three sat quietly around the table while their thoughts went in entirely different directions. No-one dared to speak as they each wrestled with the results the day had brought them so far. However there was a unanimous feeling growing among them that Johnno was right. They owed it to themselves to think of something before they returned the bottle to the sea.

"Umm, excuse me," a polite voice interrupted their thoughts. "Would you be interested in buying a ticket in our annual lifeguard fundraiser?"

The three looked up to see a young girl, no older than eighteen, dressed in a lifeguard shirt. An I.D. tag dangled from a lanyard around her neck and in her arms she clutched a folder. Without waiting for a reply, she quickly opened the folder and thrust a colored brochure onto the table in front of them.

"It's the last day we're selling them," she said routinely. "They're ten dollars a ticket. First prize is a fully furnished luxury condo right on the beach, and it's drawn tomorrow."

Anton and Johnno looked at each other and shrugged their shoulders, each waiting for the other to say something. Finally a smile broke across their faces and they turned excitedly to the young girl who was waiting for their answer.

"Yes please," they said in unison.

"Great," the young girl said as she opened the folder and placed it down on the table in front of them. "So do you want to buy a ticket each? Or are you going to share one between all three of you?"

"We'll just share the one ticket between the three of us," Anton said with a smile on his face.

"No you don't," Tanya suddenly objected. "Don't include me in this plan of yours."

"Why not?" Anton asked her.

"Because you know where I stand when it comes to gambling," Tanya folded her arms in protest.

"But it's just a raffle ticket Tan," Anton pleaded with her. "Someone is going to win this beach condo anyway, so it may as well be us."

"You know I can't Anton. I don't believe in gambling." She stood her ground.

"But it's also the lifeguard's annual fundraiser," Anton continued. "As a Christian you believe in helping out your community don't you?"

"Yes but I'd rather make a donation than buy a raffle ticket."

"That's alright," the young girl politely interrupted their debate. "We can also accept a donation if that's what you'd rather do."

"See, she accepts donations," Tanya looked at the young girl approvingly, "and that's just what I am going to do."

"Ah, I still don't understand you after all these years," Anton sighed, watching as Tanya took five dollars from her pocket and handed it to the girl.

"I've told you a thousand times before Anton, it's exactly the same as your surfing theory. Being a Christian isn't just something you do. It's a way of life," she said and flashed a satisfied smile at him from across the table.

"So now you're going to tell me that I shouldn't buy raffle tickets aren't you," Anton sighed and slumped back in the chair.

"No, not at all," Tanya corrected him. "That would be judging others wouldn't it? And as a Christian I don't believe in that either."

"So in other words you're saying that Johnno and I should hurry up and buy the ticket before you eventually beat me into being saved," Anton said cautiously.

"One day I'm finally going to convince you that it is far better to stand for something than it is to fall for anything," she laughed.

"So are we doing this or not?" Johnno asked, growing

impatient by the simple task that was now becoming a drawn out debate.

"How much do we have between us?" Anton asked as he put his last seven dollars down on the table.

"I only have two dollars on me," Johnno said dejectedly. "My wallet is in the van."

"That's alright," Tanya interrupted the two. "Here's the other dollar you need. Just don't go putting my name on the ticket."

"We'll take one ticket please," Anton finally said to the girl who had stood waiting patiently the entire time, "on one condition."

"Okay, what's the condition?" The girl asked timidly.

"I wish you would sell the winning ticket to us," Johnno said the words carefully.

"Oh right," the girl tried to laugh politely. "If I had a dollar for every time someone said that to me."

The girl collected the money and the two boys wrote their names carefully on the stub of the ticket. Finally the girl tore the ticket from the book and left it on the table in front of them, before thanking them for their support and moving on to the next table to repeat the whole process again.

"Hey everybody, they've just re-opened the beach. Let's go play some volleyball," a young guy in board shorts suddenly called out in excitement from the entrance to the café. Immediately a cheer went up from the table of bikini-clad girls.

Johnno watched sadly as they all rose to their feet and began to file out of the café. Only to divert his gaze quickly when he thought Tanya had looked disapprovingly in his direction. A part of him still wondered if what she had said to him earlier today had been true. Or would it be a case of her reverting to her normal self tonight after they returned the bottle to the sea?

"So you're a Christian?" Johnno turned and asked Tanya once the crowd had emptied out of the café.

177

"That's right," she answered, sounding a little surprised by Johnno's question. "Didn't Anton ever mention it to you?"

"I'm afraid not," Johnno said as he looked disappointedly in Anton's direction.

"Hey dude, I thought you would have worked that out for yourself by now," Anton said as he put his hands up in protest. "It should have been obvious."

"Yeah, I guess you're right," Johnno thought aloud. "It all makes perfect sense now."

"I don't understand. What makes perfect sense?" Tanya asked, suddenly concerned by the possibility of there being some hidden meaning to his statement.

"Nothing," Johnno added quickly. "I didn't mean for it to sound bad. It's just that you've always seemed like such a nice person."

"Why thank you," Tanya replied.

"So that's why I've never been able to understand why you haven't been nice to me in the past," Johnno continued. "Now I understand, I've probably said a lot of things to offend you."

"No, not at all," Tanya apologized. "I'm sorry if I've given you that impression. I actually like you a lot. It's just that I wanted to keep whatever feelings I had for you under control. Now I can see now that I've probably acted rudely at times. I'm sorry, but I'm the one who should be apologizing."

"Ah, that's okay. It's all water under the bridge now," Johnno assured her. "But how can you explain everything that has happened today because of the poem you put in the bottle? Would God really let something like this happen for no reason?"

"You're forgetting one thing dude," Anton interrupted him. "Her God was the one who gave Moses the power to part the Red Sea, Noah the instructions to build an ark and then raised Jesus from the dead. You think He can't give a young girl's letter the power to make a wish come true? Maybe He did so purely to teach us all a lesson."

178

"I guess you're right Anton," Tanya agreed. Only she felt guilty that her lack of Faith was now being reassured in the most unlikely of ways, through her non-Christian friends. "But I don't know if God caused this to happen, or if it is all just a series of ill-timed coincidences. I'm sure that if He did allow everything that has happened today to take place, then He did so for a reason. Perhaps by the end of the day we each would have learnt a valuable lesson."

Had she ever stopped to think of what impact her Faith could make in the lives of others if she put their concerns ahead of her own? When she wasn't being angry at God for taking away those she had loved most in her life, she was busy being annoyed at Him for failing to introduce her to Mr Right. Now she shared a quiet table in the café listening to her best friend Anton defending God to the man that she so desperately wanted to be Mr Right. And what had she done? She'd succeeded in treating Johnno rudely for the past two years because to share the Gospel with him meant the risk of being rejected in two different ways, both spiritually and emotionally. It seemed that she did have something to learn after all.

"Well, what do we do now?" Johnno sighed as he sank back into the chair.

"I don't know dude. But I'm flat broke," Anton threw his hands in the air and laughed.

"Seven dollars?" Tanya asked in disbelief. "If that was all the money you had, then you need this job more than I thought."

"So there you have it. Now that we've thought of something to wish for that isn't going to hurt anyone, this is all out of our hands," Johnno said, feeling the weight of responsibility fall from his shoulders. "We'll put the letter back in the bottle and take it with us when we go surfing. After we paddle out on our boards we'll make sure we toss it way out into the sea."

"That sounds good dude. Only you're forgetting one thing."

"What's that?" Johnno asked.

"The meeting we're supposed to go to this afternoon at the holiday park."

"I almost forgot. That's at half past three isn't it?" Johnno glanced at the clock on the wall of the café. "I wish I knew what it was about."

"I'm sure we'll find out soon enough without you having to make any more wishes." Anton chuckled. "Besides the letter did say to return it to the sea at sunset, I think we can wait until after the meeting before we take it surfing with us."

"Well surely you boys have time to have a cup of coffee before you head off," Tanya proposed as she stood to her feet. "Come on Johnno, you can give me a hand while Anton saves the table for us. And don't worry Anton. I'm paying for this one."

Johnno only smiled in return as he stood up, but deep down he didn't want his wish for Tanya to like him to end at sunset. He now wanted what she had said earlier today to be true.

3.20pm

For what it's worth

"Why do you think all the cars are here?" Johnno asked as he pulled the Kombi van to the side of the road about fifty feet short of the entrance to the trailer park.

"Beats me dude," Anton said as he peered through the windscreen at the large crowd that had gathered out front of the Kings Beach Holiday Park, "but we're not going to be able to park any closer than this."

Johnno cut the engine and stepped out. Letting the door of the Volkswagen Kombi slam shut behind him. In front of the trailer park a TV news crew had set up in the driveway. It was the same TV broadcast van that had earlier today covered the tragedy of the construction worker who had fallen from the scaffolding on the construction site. It was also the same TV crew who had their cameras rolling when the rent-a-loo had fallen on the site manager. Now Johnno could recognize the female reporter running toward him with the cameraman in tow. It was the same reporter who had interviewed him only hours earlier following the accident at the beach.

"Hi remember me from earlier today?" She asked quickly as the cameraman positioned his camera behind her. "Do you live here? Am I able to ask you a few quick questions?"

"Umm, yeah I live here," Johnno answered, taken aback by all the attention. "I live in one of the trailers inside the park. What's wrong?"

"That's great," she brushed his question aside. "Now I'm sorry to have to ask, but what is your name again?"

"John." He looked puzzled as to why she would want to talk with him again. "My name is John Clark, and this is my friend Anton. He also lives in the park."

"That's great. But it is you I'd like to interview," she said with a sense of urgency. "Now if I can get your friend to step aside for a moment we need to get the cameras rolling."

"Umm, okay I guess," Johnno said as Anton was moved out of the way by the female reporter and left to stand behind the man with the camera.

"John how does it feel after everything you've endured today to return to the trailer park you call home only to find out it is about to be torn down and replaced with a block of luxury waterfront condominiums?"

"What? Are you serious?" He looked blankly at the reporter. "When did they decide this?"

"In the eyes of a true local hero, do you feel today's announcement will leave many of the park's residents feeling angry that they were not first consulted prior to today's meeting."

"This is the first mention I've heard of such a thing. I'm shocked. What are we supposed to do if they close the park and kick us all out?" He asked in return.

Amongst the confusion that gripped his mind he looked in Anton's direction, trying to get a better indication of what was happening. Anton however seemed just as stunned by the revelation as him.

"There must seem a sense of prevailing injustice to think that the many people who ignored the cries for help at the scene of an accident earlier today, choosing instead to loot large amounts of cash from the scene while you bravely rescued three men, are at home now counting their money while you are about to be evicted from yours?"

Johnno had to think quickly for an answer. It was surely the longest question he had ever been asked in his life. Quite possibly it may have been the longest question ever asked in the history of the world.

"Umm yeah, I guess you could say that," he replied.

"Okay, that will have to do it," the reporter thanked him. "They are just about to make the announcement."

With those few words, Johnno's five seconds of fame were over. It wasn't exactly what he had in mind when earlier this morning he had wished he was famous on TV.

"What is this all about dude?" Anton asked the minute the cameraman had stepped out of the way.

"How would I know?" Johnno looked at him. "But I'd like to ask Mal the same question. I thought something was wrong yesterday when he asked us all to this meeting."

"Yeah, well just remember you wished you knew what this meeting is all about," Anton chuckled at the irony, "and now you know."

Anton and Johnno shuffled their way towards the small circle of chairs that were set up in front of the reception office. In the front row sat a handful of business men in long-sleeved shirts, and women dressed in neatly pressed blouses, black skirts and pantyhose. They looked ridiculously overdressed on what had been such a hot summer's day. Behind them lurked a crowd of park residents. Their faces thick with the disgruntled look of people who had just been dragged away from their favorite afternoon TV shows.

"Ladies and gentlemen, can I have your attention please? We'd like to get this meeting underway," a well-groomed businessman in a black suit spoke into a microphone connected to a portable amplifier that had been set up especially for the occasion.

Anton noticed the lonely figure of Mal, the holiday park owner, hiding in the background under the shade of a tree. He thought about approaching him and demanding to know what was going on, but then he caught sight of the two police officers standing nearby and decided it was better not to. Instead he listened to the man in the black suit address the crowd with his boring monologue of changing seasons, what values his company held high and his thoughts on the general betterment of the community.

"Let me say I understand many of the long-term residents of the park may be saddened by today's announcement of the closure of Kings Beach Holiday Park. In recognition of this, the company wants to give each of you the opportunity to be a part of the exciting development that will be its replacement."

He paused as he turned over a large cardboard display poster that showed a map of the proposed development and a small round of applause erupted. Largely from the few businessman and women seated in the white plastic chairs.

"Now I can't say anymore about the features of these exceptionally planned resort style condos, the details won't be made public until a special meeting to launch the project tomorrow. We just wanted to come down here today at the request of Mal and ensure you that we as a company are sensitive to the needs of each and every resident."

"Enough with the baloney already," a grumpy looking man in his fifties suddenly called out, before turning to stare at Mal who was now standing beside the police officer. "How long have we got to get out Mal?"

"Let me say the company is prepared to make a special offer for any park resident who is looking to secure a stake in this spectacular development." The man in the black suit tried to take control of the situation once more. "We will pay five thousand dollars on your behalf towards the deposit on a two or three bedroom condominium of your choice, with no interest or repayments until completion."

"I'm not talking to you," the same grumpy old man shouted back. "Take a good look at all of us. I can't even afford to buy myself new clothes, and you want to sell me a luxury condo. We'll have nowhere to live once you shut this place down. Boy you sure are talking to the wrong crowd. Mal, why don't you get up here yourself and tell us exactly what is going on."

Mal stepped forward, a little apprehensively at first. Bringing a slow clap of hands from the grumpy old man, until one by one the park residents all joined in. The man in the black suit sensing the crowd had turned against him could think of nothing more to say, so reluctantly stood aside to let Mal take the microphone from him.

"I'm sorry this has come as a shock to so many of you," he began. "I've been running this place on my own for a long time now. I know a lot of faces that have been around as long as I have, but the holiday park isn't getting any younger and quite frankly neither am I. There are a lot of things in need of repair or replacement, and it seems it has reached the point where I haven't the money or desire to do anything about it. I'm sorry to disappoint so many people. But the offer came along and I thought it was the right time to sell, simple as that. I want to retire folks, not watch this place fall apart slowly over the next ten years and wish I'd have taken the opportunity when it came along."

"So how long do we have to find somewhere else to live?" Anton asked, feeling a touch embarrassed when every head turned in his direction.

"The developers want to start clearing the site in thirty days."

"Thirty days?" The grumpy old man shook his fist at the man in the black suit still standing beside Mal. "What sort of notice is that?"

"Actually a tenant legally only has to be given two weeks'

notice prior to eviction." The black-suited man briefly interrupted. "The developers have kindly reached an agreement with the park owner in which you will not be required to pay rent, effective immediately. In return for each of you signing an agreement in which you recognize that you must vacate the park within the next thirty days."

A hushed murmur rose from those gathered in front of the reception office as the concerned residents began discussing what options they had. Mal took the microphone one last time and faced the crowd, waiting until those gathered fell silent once more.

"For what it's worth, I hope we can all get together one last time for a barbeque before people start moving out. I also know that many of you are not in the position to entertain thoughts of buying a luxury waterfront condo. The developers only made the offer at my request, so I hope I didn't offend anyone by it. If anyone is interested there will be some information passed around now along with an agreement to vacate your trailer site. You'll need to sign the form if you want the next thirty day's rent waived by the developers."

"And what if we don't sign it?" The same grumpy old man spoke up, somewhat disappointed that the meeting by now hadn't erupted into an ugly scene in front of the TV camera.

The same man in the black suit stepped up to the microphone once more. Only this time he didn't address the crowd. Instead he kept his focus trained solely on the boisterous troublemaker in the faded blue singlet.

"No-one has to sign the form," he spoke calmly. "But tomorrow there will be standard fourteen day eviction notices issued for those who haven't, and you will still be required to pay rent."

Anton turned to face his solemn looking friend who had now experienced losing his job, being dumped by a girl and finally being evicted all in the one day. Somehow the look of despair spread across Johnno's face only made Anton smile. The smile turned into a grin and from that grin came the surreal sound of laughter. The crowd stopped their animated conversations and now turned to observe with some suspicion the odd sight of a man laughing moments after learning he had thirty days to vacate his home.

"Stop it Anton. You're embarrassing us," Johnno whispered hoarsely at him. "Besides, what could possibly be funny right now?"

"It's a good thing that we just bought the winning ticket in the lifeguard's fundraiser."

4.00pm

There's a storm coming

Tanya strolled leisurely along the beach on her way to meet the boys at the café. Shortly after they had left for the meeting at the trailer park, she had decided to return to her apartment and change out of her work uniform. She felt rejuvenated in a fresh change of clothes and was enjoying the feeling of the water rushing over her feet as she walked along the water's edge. The late afternoon breeze was now pleasant and cool. It made for a stark comparison to the stifling heat that they had all endured throughout the day. As always, it seemed that whenever there was a chance of an afternoon storm, it would only arrive after she had finished work for the day.

She watched the lightning in the distance as it splintered from the dark clouds that choked the horizon. Within the hour, the last remaining patch of blue summer sky would be swallowed up by the approaching storm. Perhaps even sooner she thought as a strong wind began to pick up from offshore, bringing down the beach umbrellas of hardy beachgoers who up until now had been enjoying the last official day of summer. On cue, they began packing up in droves. It seemed summer was about to make an exodus from Kings Beach for another year, only a little earlier than anticipated.

"Tanya," the voice from behind surprised her.

Turning around she came face to face once more with Kim. She was the last person she expected to see again, and to be perfectly honest she was also the last person she *wanted* to see right now.

"Kim, what a surprise," she feigned interest. "What are you doing here?"

"Why looking for John of course," she replied bluntly. "I was supposed to meet him here at four o'clock. Have you seen him?"

"As a matter of fact I have," Tanya's voice now sounded cold. "Perhaps you saw him on the TV after he rescued those three men from the accident you caused."

"I caused?" Kim grew irate. "What do you mean, I caused?"

"Oh please, Johnno told me everything that happened because of your wish. But I think what really opened his eyes as to what kind of person you are, was that you chose to steal all that money instead of stopping to help someone in need."

"I didn't steal that money. I found it," Kim protested. "While he was busy helping the men in the accident I got enough for the both of us."

"Then why did you hurt Johnno by saying such unkind things to him?"

"I only said what I did because he was being foolish for not listening to me," she answered defiantly. "Anyway, why did he tell you what I said to him? How is this any of your business?"

"Because he's with me now," Tanya lied. "He said it didn't take him long to see that you weren't the person he should be with."

A part of her felt bad for telling a lie. But playing the part of the nice Christian girl had got her nowhere when it came to men. In fact, it only created the opportunity for girls like Kim to walk all over her and steal the man from right under her nose. Well that wasn't going to happen today.

"Really?" Kim seemed disturbed by what she was hearing. "When did he say that?"

189

"When you didn't return from your lunch break, I believe it was shortly after you told him that you weren't his girlfriend."

"Oh right. I guess I owe the manager an explanation for taking the afternoon off," she admitted. "And I probably need to explain what I said earlier to John."

"I wouldn't bother if I were you Kim." Tanya tried to hide the spite in her voice, only it wasn't working. "Jake gave your job to Anton this afternoon and Johnno said he never wanted to see you again. It would probably be best if you just walked away and saved yourself the hurt and embarrassment. Johnno and I are together now and there's nothing you can do that will change it."

"Well I just want to say..." Kim thought about continuing her argument with Tanya. Only if what she was saying were true, then what would be the point of leaving herself open to the hurt that would surely follow?

"There's nothing left to say Kim," Tanya calmly offered some false comfort. "But I'm sure things will work out for you."

"Well if I can't be with John..." Kim tried vainly to aim her anger at Tanya, but she could only do her best to be heard through the tearful sobs that began to erupt. "Then I wish you couldn't be with John either."

Kim sadly trudged off along the beach, disappearing into the stormy afternoon. Tanya, feeling satisfied for staking her claim on the man she was sure she loved, turned the other way and hurried towards the café. Anton and Johnno had promised they would meet her there as soon as the meeting at the trailer park was over. Ignoring the approaching storm and the swarm of beachgoers leaving the beach, she also ignored Kim's tearful last words.

Tonight at her birthday party she was going to make sure that Johnno would be hers, all hers. The other details would then take care of themselves. Surely God would understand.

4.15pm

Sand beneath my feet

The beach was a mess by the time Johnno steered the Kombi van into the parking lot. At least there was no problem with finding a parking space. Most of the beachgoers had finished packing up and were in the process of filing out of the parking lot and scurrying back to the comfort of their holiday apartments on account of the weather turning nasty. The parking lot was almost deserted. Small swirls of sand drifted in from the beach and danced their way across the empty spaces like mini tornados. Very soon the parking lot would resemble the beach itself. Sand was already piling up against the kerbing and the tires of the few vehicles that were still parked here. No doubt there would still be a few diehard surfers out in the water, enjoying the near cyclonic conditions that had whipped the sea into a frenzied mess.

Anton looked across at the café as he grabbed the bottle from out of his backpack and stepped out of the van. The courtyard outside Mermaids was deserted. The tables and chairs were all packed up. Stacked neatly inside and locked away behind the thick glass doors that were shut tight. The side door that was partly opened was the only indication that inside, the café was still open for business. One thing was for sure, this was not the afternoon to be enjoying coffee by the beach.

The two boys hurried across the windswept parking lot, feeling the sting of the sand that lashed their ankles and reached the sanctuary of the café. The air from the giant blower above the door was freezing cold as they stepped underneath it, leaving both to wish that they had at least worn a t-shirt. Instead they stood in the doorway of the café wearing only board shorts and a layer of goose bumps across their chests.

"There you are," Tanya called from their usual table the moment she saw them.

Anton and Johnno hurried over to where she sat waiting for them. There was only one other couple sitting inside, watching as some TV anchorman broadcast a severe weather warning for the entire stretch of coastline.

"Have you got everything we talked about earlier?" Anton asked as he sat down opposite her.

"It's all here," she pointed to the objects lined up on the table, then smiled warmly as Johnno sat down beside her. "How did the meeting go?"

"The holiday park has been sold to a bunch of developers," Johnno sighed, still obviously disappointed by the announcement. "All the residents have been given thirty days notice to get out."

"That's terrible," she said as she placed her hand on his arm. "I guess you'll be hoping that you do win the beach condo tomorrow after all."

"That's what I said," Anton laughed as he placed the bottle in the middle of the table.

"Well let's just return your letter to the sea Tanya and hope that we're right," Johnno said as he rolled up the letter he had been holding in his hand and reached across to put it back in the bottle.

"No wait!" Tanya stopped him before the letter had the chance to fall down inside its glass neck. "You're supposed to write something on the blank page first."

192

"Like what?" Johnno asked.

"Like a message from you to whoever finds it next," she said eagerly. "It only has to be a few words. Something like you would normally write in a birthday card."

"Okay, do you have a pen?" Johnno asked as he unrolled the letter once more and stared at the blank page.

Tanya who was already prepared for the question simply slid a pen along the table. Without taking too long to think about what he would write, Johnno instinctively picked up the pen and wrote; *'Greetings from Kings Beach, Johnno'* and passed the pen and the letter to Anton.

"That's it?" Tanya looked at him in disbelief.

"I wanted to make sure I left room for the next person to write something," Johnno said as he smiled warmly at the pretty, brown-eyed blonde who sat beside him. "Perhaps they'll have better luck at figuring out what to wish for than we did."

"There, now we can lay this poem to rest and return the bottle to the ocean before sunset," Anton said as he put the pen and paper down on the table in front of him.

"What did you write?" Tanya asked curiously.

"Does it matter?" He asked growing more impatient by the minute. "I'm starting to worry that if we take any longer to do this, we won't get that bottle back in the water without it washing straight back onto the shore."

Tanya picked up what was once a blank page and read the words he had written beside Johnno's message; *'Be careful what you wish for, Anton.'*

"I like it," she said approvingly, "and to answer your question, yes it does matter. This is probably the only time I will actually get to see what someone has written after they find it."

"Well what are we waiting for? Let's seal the bottle and throw it back," Anton said as though concluding a meeting. "We all have a birthday party to get to."

In front of them, Tanya had already laid out everything that

Anton had asked her to prepare earlier that afternoon before he'd left for the meeting at the trailer park. Beside the pen which had already performed its part, there was a cork she had salvaged from an opened wine bottle in the kitchen, a small jar of Vaseline, a paper plate, a candle and a box of matches. The three stared at the letter one last time. Johnno then rolled the letter tightly until it could fit easily through the neck of the bottle, reached over and let it land inside with a soft thud.

Tanya greased the cork with the Vaseline so that it slid back into the neck of the bottle with only a little bit of force. The Vaseline would also help repel any water from seeping into the bottle and spoiling the letter. Anton took the matches and lit the candle. Once the flame had grown to its full height he then held the bottle out over the paper plate and tilted the candle. The three watched as the wax dripped slowly over the cork. Any drops that missed fell noisily onto the paper plate beneath it until it seemed the neck of the bottle was completely sealed from any chance of water getting inside. Finally Anton stood the bottle on the table and held the candle up in front of Tanya.

"I think it's only fair that the birthday girl should get to make a wish," he said.

Tanya closed her eyes, thought hard for a moment and then blew the candle out. The wick smoldered silently in the room, leaving a tiny plume of smoke in its wake.

"Now if you'll excuse me for just a moment, I need to pay a quick visit to the men's room," Anton announced as he stood to his feet.

"Must you?" Johnno groaned in protest.

"I'm sorry but the air-conditioning is so cold that I can't hold on any longer," Anton said before he hurried quickly in the direction of the restroom.

Tanya waited until Anton had disappeared from sight before she turned nervously to face Johnno. His skin looked so cold and taunt that she wanted to put her arms around him to warm him up.

"Do you know what I wished for?" She tried her best to look seductive. Only it was a look she hadn't practiced much at all, so she really wasn't sure how effective it appeared to the man sitting beside her.

"Umm, I think the idea is that you aren't supposed to tell anyone what you wished for," Johnno said as he squirmed uncomfortably. He still didn't know if her feelings toward him were genuine, or simply the result of his earlier wish for Tanya to like him.

"Well I need to tell you if I'm to have any chance of it coming true," she said while playing with her hair.

He swallowed.

"I guess in that case you'll have to tell me."

"I wished that tonight before my birthday party is over, you would kiss me," she blushed at the words that were coming out of her own mouth. What would her mother think of such promiscuous behavior?

"Really?" Johnno's nerves caused his body to start shaking. Or was it the fact that the air-conditioning was so darn cold?

"I've spent my whole life trying to live up to the memories of people who knew me as sweet and innocent. Well guess what? I'm not a little girl anymore," she said as she tried to stop her hands from shaking. "That's the reason I wrote the poem and put it in the bottle. I want to be free from the fear of letting people down for admitting I have feelings for a man who isn't a Christian."

"Whoa, are you serious?" Johnno could hardly believe what he had just heard. "So everything you said to me earlier is true. You've felt this way about me before today, haven't you?"

"Yes I have," she said determinedly, brushing aside years of inhibition and seizing the moment with both hands. "Obviously you now know that I'm a Christian and I still firmly believe in saving sex for marriage, but I can't deny my feelings anymore. I'm only hoping I can find a way for us to make this work without jeopardising my relationship with God by dating someone who is a non-believer."

"Wow. Look as flattered as I am Tanya, I think there's something you should know," he began.

"What is it?" She interrupted. Her face was still red from the embarrassment of what she had just said. "Did I say it the wrong way? Is it me? You don't want to kiss me?"

"No it's not that at all," he said as he placed his hand reassuringly on hers. The sensation of her smooth skin sent tiny shockwaves of electricity racing up his arm. "Look, I don't know what sort of guy you think I am, but I'm…"

"Oh my goodness, are you gay?"

"No, of course not!" He scoffed at the thought. "Why do women always jump to that conclusion?"

"Then what is it?" She looked at him with piercing brown eyes that demanded an answer.

"It's just that I'm a virgin too," he whispered softly.

"You're a virgin?" She almost shouted in disbelief, causing the couple who were still sitting at the far end of the room to turn around and stare curiously in their direction.

"Okay, can you keep it down a little?" Johnno asked as he sunk back into the chair. "It wasn't a conscious decision that I made, it just sort of turned out that way."

"But I thought you would have been with lots of women."

"Why would you think that?" Johnno looked at her carefully. "Besides, what makes you think I don't believe in God?"

"You do?" She looked confused.

"Of course I do."

"How long have you been a believer?"

"Since I was five and my parents would make me go to Sunday school."

"But I've never heard you mention anything that would give

196

me the impression that you might be a Christian." Tanya stopped to take in this latest surprise. "Do you still go to Church?"

"No. I haven't been to Church since I was twelve years old," Johnno admitted. "My parents went from thinking that Sunday school was the best thing for me at a young age, to pushing me to get good grades at school. I guess somewhere along the way it just got forgotten about."

"That's so sad."

"Not really," he thought. "I've still lived my life trying to do the right thing when it counted. Like today when the accident happened on the beach. You know, it's that whole do unto others as you'd have them do to you thing. Surely that counts for something."

"But it's much more than just that Johnno. It's your relationship with God. Here I am worrying about finding a relationship that could last a lifetime, when you've been missing out on a relationship with God that could last an eternity." She slouched back into the chair beside him and let a single sigh escape her mouth. "I've been so obsessed with controlling my feelings toward you that I've failed to see the bigger picture that God has put in front of me. Is it just me? Or have I totally gone about this the wrong way?"

"I think I should return this bottle to the sea," Johnno said as he took her hand and held it gently in his. "Then tonight, after the sun has set, perhaps I could start by asking you to dance with me at your party."

"I think I'd like that," she said before her head turned and their eyes locked on each others.

For one brief flickering moment in time, Johnno felt his head moving slowly towards hers, as though guided by the glimmer of promise that danced in her eyes. The longing he felt to press his lips against hers caused his heart to catch in his throat. He thought he saw her eyes move to close, and then Anton returned.

"Okay dude. Let's grab the bottle and we'll close the chapter on this book," he said loudly before slapping Johnno on the back.

"Do you mean now?" Johnno asked as he felt the moment slip away.

"Of course I mean now," Anton said in disbelief. "There's a huge storm brewing outside and we've only got a few minutes to do this before it hits. Right now I should be feeling the sand beneath my feet instead of the cold tiled floor."

"Okay. Let's do this," he said as he felt Tanya's hand slip from under his. He stood up, grabbed the bottle from the table and turned to look at Tanya once more. "I'll see you tonight at your party."

4.30pm

Last Wish of Summer

"Anton, grab your board and let's go!" Johnno shouted above the wind. "The surf is really pumping man."

"Are you sure you really want to go out in this?" Anton asked as he hurried to where Johnno stood waiting at the back of the van. "It looks rough dude. We'll never be able to paddle out in this size swell."

"We've been waiting for some decent sized waves all summer and you want to chicken out now?" Johnno poked fun at him. "Besides, we have to paddle out past the breakers to throw the bottle out to sea."

Anton looked around at the deserted beach. The scene looked like something straight out of a disaster movie. Leaves and small branches fell from the trees and blew across the grass in the empty park in front of the beach. The few shops along the beach strip had all closed early and any loose objects had been locked away inside, just as the weather report on the TV broadcast had recommended.

"I don't know dude," Anton said as he scratched his head nervously. "I don't know if I'm up for it."

"Don't be stupid," Johnno said as he placed a hand on his shoulder and gently shook him. "These are the days we live for. I've never seen the surf this big before. Unless you can wish a way for us to go to Hawaii and surf Pipeline, we may never see waves this big again. Trust me. We'll be talking about this afternoon for a very, very long time."

"Okay dude," Anton said. "I'll give it a try. But if I don't like it, I'm coming straight back in."

"There you go buddy!" Johnno punched him on the shoulder. "You only live once."

"What if it rains though?" Anton asked as he took his surfboard out of the back of the Kombi. "I don't want to stand around getting drenched while I wait for you to come in."

"I'll leave the back tailgate unlocked. You can get your towel, put your board in the back and climb inside," Johnno answered him. "Anyway, we'll only be out there long enough to throw the bottle as far out into the ocean as we can. So what do you say?"

Johnno took his board out of the back, wedged the bottle under his armpit and closed the tailgate on the Volkswagen. Anton followed him uneasily across the parking lot that was now covered in a thin layer of sand. The wind continued to gust in from across the ocean and blow the sand hard up against the small fence that acted as a wind barrier at the top of the beach. Small dunes were forming across the sidewalk wherever there was a gap in the fence and some sections of the wind barrier were almost completely buried in the sand as it continued its relentless march inland. The once green and grassy park now resembled a patchwork quilt of sandy top-dressed lawn, with only the tips of the blades visible in some places.

The ocean roared menacingly in the background above the sound of the wind. Even the sight of the gray, threatening skies that had gathered overhead could not prepare them for the sight of the ocean as they stepped down onto the sand. The shoreline was completely white from the foam that had been churned up from the incessant pounding of the waves against the shore. Beyond it were massive walls of menacing gray water that rose nearly ten feet above the stormy sea before crumbling and finally crashing on the shore.

Anton walked uneasily across the sand, unsure if he wanted to venture out into the freakishly huge surf. By the time he'd reached the water's edge however, his friend had already strapped on his leg rope and was ready to paddle out to where half a dozen other surfers were risking life and limb to paddle over each monstrous wave.

"Come on. Let's do this!" Johnno shouted as he wedged the bottle down the front of his board shorts. "I can't think of a better way to say goodbye to summer than catching one of these monsters."

"I can," Anton said hesitantly. "Besides, I already said goodbye to summer half an hour ago when the weather turned bad."

"Once you're out there you'll feel fine," Johnno tried to reassure him.

"What about the bottle?" Anton pointed to the wine bottle that was wedged down the front of his board shorts. "Isn't that a little dangerous? What if it breaks and cuts you?"

Johnno looked down at the glass bottle and simply repositioned it closer to his hip.

"Unless you can think of a better way I'll just have to be careful," he reasoned.

Johnno then turned and ran out into the water. His surfboard was tucked firmly under one arm while his other free hand clutched the bottle that was wedged down the front of his board shorts. Anton watched as his friend's legs begin to slow from the onslaught of white water. Then in one swift motion, he gently dropped down onto his surfboard and began to paddle out in complete disregard for his own safety. Johnno paused again and again as he dove under each wall of churning water that raced towards the shore. When Anton was satisfied that his friend had emerged safely each time, he too followed.

The first wall of white water hit him hard as he raced head-first into the angry sea. With no time to dive beneath it, Anton slammed into the churning mass of foam and felt it pull him back towards the shore. He clenched his teeth hard and began to paddle furiously into the onslaught, determined to follow Johnno's path towards the open water. As the next wall of white water raced toward him, Anton plunged beneath the surface. He could feel the force of what remained from the wave shake his whole body as it passed over him. He repeated this again and again, wondering how on earth Johnno was able to do this with a wine bottle tucked down the front of his pants. After feeling that he was going nowhere, he finally caught a small break between the sets of onrushing waves, and paddled furiously until he left the churning white water behind.

Anton looked up and swallowed hard. He'd thought that the surf looked menacing when he was on the shore, but now that he found himself looking up at a ten foot wave that was about to come crashing down on him, it was just plain scary. He drew a huge breath and dove under.

The water suddenly felt icy cold as he disappeared deep beneath the surface, holding on to his board with all his might. His body rocked violently as the wave passed over him, until finally he emerged behind the monstrous wave just when it felt like his lungs would burst. He gasped for air, feeling the sudden crash of the wave behind him reverberate through the water like a bomb being detonated. And then it happened. He felt like he was stuck in slow motion as the sickening feeling of being sucked backwards overpowered him. The wave sucked him back into its grip, pulling him under and sending him hurtling underwater with the force of a washing machine on steroids.

When he finally escaped the wave's grip and emerged once more on the surface, he had exactly ten seconds to find his surfboard, climb back on and try to make it over the next wave that was already racing towards him. It wasn't enough time.

Anton gripped his board in fear as he felt himself being lifted up into the air. There was nothing to do but hope for a safe landing as the wave threw him in front and came crashing down around him. He held his breath underwater for longer than he ever had in his lifetime, luckily escaping from being hit by the surfboard that now tugged angrily at the strap around his ankle. When he came to the surface once more, there was only a smaller wave in front of him that he easily floated over the top of. That left him with enough time to scramble back onto his board, cough up a mouthful of saltwater and clench his teeth with determination before he paddled head-first into the next set of much bigger waves that followed.

Anton paddled like there was no tomorrow. He had to beat the next wave or he'd find himself going over the falls again. It rose up in front of him like an evil giant, staring down at Anton like he was a pathetic mortal for daring to paddle directly into its path. There was going to be no prize for second place Anton thought as he paddled furiously towards the wave. He was either going to win, or pay the price for trying.

The wave met him head on. Anton continued to paddle hard as it began to lift him up. His arms hurt as he commanded his body to make each desperate stroke. His lungs ached from trying to suck in as much oxygen as he could. The wave continued to lift him up, up, up until finally he felt himself falling, over the other side and free from its grasp.

Anton breathed a sigh of relief. He had made it. As he continued to paddle into the open water he rolled effortlessly over the next two approaching waves. Finally he could see Johnno sitting leisurely on his board, no more than twenty feet from a small group of other surfers who watched and waited for the perfect wave to come along.

"What took you so long?" He joked as Anton paddled wearily towards him. "I was beginning to think you'd changed your mind."

"I was beginning to think I wasn't going to make it," Anton

panted heavily as he drew alongside before dropping his head down on his board from exhaustion.

"Well don't rest just yet," Johnno said as he waved the bottle for Anton to see. "We have to wish our little friend a safe journey to wherever in the world it is going to."

"My guess is Hawaii," Anton joked.

"We may never know," Johnno seemed intrigued by the thought. "I do know one thing though."

"What's that?"

"If you wanted to make another wish," he said as he held the bottle proudly. "Now would be your last chance."

"No more wishes dude," Anton said as he continued to suck in as much air as he could. "Just let me catch my breath."

"Okay man. But don't take all day. There's a killer storm coming our way."

Johnno pointed towards the southern end of the beach and Anton turned to look at the storm clouds that were brewing as black as coffee in the distance. Above them the sky had turned an eerie, pale gray color and the wind was beginning to pick up stronger than it had been on shore.

"Well, let's do this," Anton said as he sat up and straddled his surfboard. "Let's put an end to all this nonsense and hope that everything returns to normal tomorrow."

"Do you want to do it?" Johnno asked.

"What does it matter?" Anton looked across at his friend. "Just throw it out as far as you can and we'll catch a wave into shore."

"But we just got out here."

"And judging by the clouds that are headed our way, it's time to leave."

"Okay," Johnno said as he gripped the bottle tightly in his hand. "But before I do, I just want to make one more wish. I wish for one more big wave, something that we'll be talking about for the rest of our lives. That's my last wish of summer."

With that said, he threw the bottle with all his might. Anton watched as it left his hand and sailed into the air. The bottle with the colorful dots all painted in a row that once more contained nothing but a heartfelt poem. Yet somehow it had managed to turn an otherwise ordinary day into what could still be easily mistaken as a series of amazing coincidences. It floated high in the air for a few glorious seconds, and then fell gracelessly into the cold, gray sea and was gone.

"Okay. I guess that is that," Anton said after watching for a moment for any sign of the bottle bobbing in the ocean.

"Where did it go? Did it sink?" Johnno seemed confused as to why he couldn't see it in the distance.

"I don't think so," Anton guessed as he tried to see over the crest of each rolling wave. "But we're never going to be able to see it when the water is this choppy. Now let's get that wave and go to shore."

"Okay here we go," Johnno said excitedly as he eyed a huge wave that was rolling towards them.

Anton watched his friend paddle confidently into position and then gasped as the wave began to pick him up. As Anton floated safely up and over the wave, he caught sight of Johnno getting to his feet as he dropped down on the other side. It was only a quick glance, and then he was gone. From behind the wave, Anton watched for any sign of his friend as the wind whipped a huge spray of water into the air. Finally he appeared. As though timed to perfection, he shot high into the air as the wave collapsed beneath him, clutching his board with one hand as he crouched down and made a soft landing behind the wave and out of harm's way.

It was a maneuver that they had practiced endlessly in smaller conditions, but never to the effect that Johnno had just pulled off.

"How good was that?" Johnno hollered as he paddled over to where Anton sat watching. "Just make sure you pull out before it breaks, that way you won't get stuck trying to paddle back out here again through all the white water."

"Well here goes. Wish me luck," Anton said as he lined up an approaching wave and tried to put on a brave face.

"Hasn't today taught you anything?" Johnno laughed. "Besides, we don't have the bottle anymore. So making a wish now is just a waste of time."

Anton felt the wave rise beneath him. His arms still ached from having paddled out this far but he did enough to put himself in the right position and get to his feet just as the wave built to a peak behind him. There were no perfect barrels or clean, smooth surfaces to glide down this afternoon. Only the full fury of an angry sea to harness as you hung on for dear life. One slip on a wave this size and it was game over. Anton could see the ocean floor draining in front of him. As though ten feet of water behind him wasn't enough power to try and control, the sheer force of the wave sucked another two feet of water from beneath him. There was nothing to do but keep the board placed firmly beneath your feet and drop down into a blue-gray abyss.

The board threaded its way down the face of the wave on a sharp angle. Anton could feel every bump on the way down. The spray of saltwater that the wind was now kicking up only stung his eyes and saturated his face, making it hard to see where he was heading. Behind him the wave began to crumble, sending an avalanche of white water chasing close behind. Sensing that the huge wall was about to collapse over the top of him, Anton did as Johnno had said. Reaching the bottom of the wave, he turned sharply and pointed the board skywards. His arms flung out on either side of his body as he struggled to maintain balance. As the wave behind him tumbled down in a thunderous crash, Anton glided easily across the shoulder of the wave that was yet to break and disappeared safely over the top.

There was just enough time to drop back down onto his

stomach and paddle clear of the next wave that Johnno was ready to catch. Anton watched again as he safely rolled over the top while his friend dropped down the steeply forming side. Again the wind whipped up a huge sheet of spray as the wave passed by. The sea was growing wilder by the minute, tiny crests of white water appeared as far as the eye could see. By the time Johnno had paddled back to where Anton waited, the sky had grown dark overhead.

"Where'd the others go?" Anton yelled to Johnno as he paddled alongside him.

"They've headed into shore," Johnno shouted above the wind. "It's getting too rough out here. We'll have to head in soon. But not before I catch one last big wave."

"What's that noise?" Anton called loudly.

"It's just some thunder in the distance," Johnno shouted back. On cue, a bolt of lightning flashed from out of the black clouds that had closed in.

"No. Listen closely," Anton yelled. "It sounds like traffic noise, only it's getting louder."

The two turned and looked south along the beach. Beyond the rocks at the mouth of the river, and further south to where the beach stretched off on the other side as far as the eye could see. Only the beach was quickly being swallowed up by an approaching wall of gray that raced towards them like a speeding train.

"It's just some rain," Johnno said matter-of-factly.

"I don't like it. I'm going into shore," Anton shouted. "Let's get out of here Johnno, you don't want to be out here when that hits us."

"One more wave Anton," he shouted.

"You're crazy!" Anton yelled at him as he stared nervously at the approaching storm. "It's not worth it, get in to shore now!"

"I will okay. I'll be right behind you."

Anton turned and paddled as fast as he could towards the

shore. Behind him, the ocean quickly resembled a washing machine as the storm rushed forward. Huge peaks of water appeared from everywhere. He felt each one as it threatened to pick him up and toss him from his board. Strangely enough, he still needed to catch one to be able to make it back to shore. He looked quickly over his shoulder to where Johnno seemed to be paddling into position to catch a wave, and then he saw it.

It appeared out of nowhere, a towering mountain of water that dwarfed every other wave that he had nervously paddled over. Anton felt the color drain from his face faster than the water that drained from in front of the monster. He watched in horror as Johnno paddled directly into its path. As the wave continued to surge forward like an unstoppable beast, everything suddenly fell quiet. In that shortest of moments it felt like the earth had stopped turning. The wind subsided and the lingering smell of salt air seemed uneasily still. Anton even thought he could hear the sound of his own heart beating. And then the storm hit.

Like a jumbo jet lifting off a runway it suddenly roared overhead, bringing with it a curtain of small hailstones that mercilessly pelted Anton's bare skin. The sky became completely gray, and the sound of the hailstones striking the surface of the water was accompanied only by the roar of the huge wave that crashed somewhere behind him. Anton looked over his shoulder once more, straining his eyes desperately to see if Johnno was riding the wave to shore. Instead he was greeted with the sudden explosion of a huge wall of white water that knocked him from his board. Once more he was under water, tumbling over and over again.

The first indication Anton had that he was once more above the surface was the stinging sensation from the rain that lashed at his face. It ricocheted off the water all around him like gunshots, sending droplets of water flying back into the air. The rain caused a blinding gray haze all around him that made it impossible for him to see more than two feet in any direction. The panic that followed rose from somewhere deep inside him, from a place he didn't know existed. At first it was purely a realization of the predicament he now found himself in. Then it quickly turned into a gripping fear that sent his whole body numb. Turning around frantically while he struggled to keep his head above water, it grew impossible to fight the urge to stay calm. He couldn't tell which direction was the sea and which was the shore!

"Help!" He screamed. "Somebody help me!"

Before he even had time to see it coming, a wall of dark gray water suddenly appeared in front of his face and once more he felt himself being lifted into the air. Not knowing where his surfboard was, Anton fell forward with the full force of the wave. Halfway down, he met his board coming in the opposite direction. It struck the side of his body and he landed heavily on it. The surfboard cracked beneath his weight. Once more he was under water, feeling the now familiar tug of the leg rope on his ankle. When he finally came to the surface once more and used his leg rope to pull the surfboard towards him, there was only half of it still attached to the other end.

"Johnno!" He shouted at the top of his lungs. "Johnno, where are you?"

There was no reply.

Behind him another wall of white water suddenly sent him under again. Only this time he wasn't ready for it, and he swallowed a huge mouthful of saltwater. Holding his breath was near impossible and he suddenly sensed that he might very well drown instead of making it back to the shore. When he came to the surface again, he couldn't breathe. The saltwater that he had swallowed only made him feel as though he was choking on gas. His lungs were burning and it was near impossible for him to inhale. He looked around again in every direction as he clung desperately to the remaining half of his surfboard, but he still couldn't see more than two feet in front of him. The rain acted like a giant curtain as it fell in torrents, completely obscuring his view.

Suddenly another huge wall of dark gray water loomed up and he thought that this was it. Surely he wasn't going to survive another trip over the falls when he still couldn't catch his breath from the last one. Anton closed his eyes and clung tightly to the remaining half of his surfboard, all the while feeling himself being lifted higher and higher into the air as the huge wave took him firmly in its grasp.

"Please God, I wish I could feel the sand beneath my feet again," he spluttered, and the words came out just in time as he began to surge forward with increasing speed.

There was the brief sensation of free-falling followed by the impact of hitting the bottom. Anton felt the full weight of the wave crush down on him, pinning him firmly to what remained of his board. Water rushed over him as he tried to hold his breath and once more he found himself bouncing around inside an enormous wall of white water. Only this time it felt different. His face surfaced from the water and he spluttered wildly for air as the wave continued to push him towards shore. Anton could feel the rain lash his face once more as he rode every bump from the surge of water. Although he was still choking for air, he felt a sense of calm return to his body. He was heading towards the shore. He was going to make it. Ahead he could see the familiar outline of the beach reappear as the force of the wave subsided. The rain began to ease slightly and it was like discovering a lost city as it emerged from the fog.

The wave let go of him when he made it to where the water was only knee-deep. Anton tried to stand up but he couldn't find the strength to do so. Instead he fell forward, face first into the water.

Suddenly two big strong pairs of arms reached down and lifted him up out of the water.

210

"Hey stay with me now," a voice shouted as he felt himself being rolled over so that his face was out of the water. "It's alright. You're safe on the shore again."

Anton couldn't find the strength to reply. Instead he lay motionless in the arms of one of the other surfers who had just made it to shore in time before the storm hit. As soon as the two burly surfers had seen his gangly frame emerge from the blanket of rain, they had raced over to where he had washed up on the shore.

"Is he okay?" The other surfer asked as they dragged him clear of the water and gently lay him down on the sand.

"No. He's stopped breathing," the first surfer answered. "Go and call an ambulance."

Anton's thoughts drifted off into oblivion. Somewhere in the inner depths of his mind the clouds broke overhead and the sunlight streamed in momentarily, turning the sea into a beautiful emerald-blue color. Just in time to see the grin on Johnno's face as he raced effortlessly down the face of that monster. He could feel the warmth of the afternoon sun flicker against his skin, and then it was gone. The clouds closed in overhead and everything went dark. The last thing he remembered was the feeling of sand beneath his feet.

"Shouldn't we take him up to the surf club?" The second guy was still asking.

"There's no time," the first guy replied firmly. "I know CPR. I was a junior lifeguard once. But I need you to get an ambulance straight away. We don't know how much water he's swallowed."

"What about the other guy who was with him?"

"Notify the lifeguards. Hopefully they'll be able to spot him when the rain eases off."

The other surfer turned and sprinted across the sand towards the surf club, leaving his friend to try and resuscitate Anton. He was in bad shape. There was no response when he tried to slap his face and he definitely wasn't breathing. The guy tilted Anton's head back, placed his mouth over Anton's and blew three times, listening as each breath wheezed back out from his mouth. Nothing happened, but he did find a pulse. He blew again, following it up this time by pressing down on his chest three times.

"One, one thousand. Two, one thousand. Three, one thousand."

Anton suddenly coughed and the surfer rolled him onto his side in time for him to vomit a stomach full of seawater onto the sand. He coughed again, took a deep breath and made an effort to sit up.

"Take it easy buddy," the surfer held him back gently. "We've just dragged you unconscious from the ocean."

"I made it?" Anton asked in disbelief as he coughed up some more saltwater. "Where's Johnno?"

"Is that your friend who was with you out there?"

"Where is he?" Anton asked again as his body began to shake violently from the sudden feeling of being cold.

"We haven't seen him yet," the stranger said quietly. "The storm hit suddenly. My friend and I waited around on shore just to make sure that you both made it in safely."

Anton tried to stand up as his eyes immediately began scanning the ocean for any sign of his friend.

"Let's just take it one step at a time," the stranger stopped him from doing anything more than sitting up. "There's an ambulance on its way. You should probably let the paramedics check you over thoroughly before you even think about moving around. People can still die from drowning hours after they've been rescued if they've swallowed too much water."

"I can't just sit here," Anton said while his body continued to shake uncontrollably. "My best friend is still out there somewhere."

"How are you ever going to spot him in these conditions huh?" The surfer tried to reason with him. "We couldn't even see you from the shore until you finally got spat out onto the sand. I'm sure that he's still on his way into shore. When did you last see him?"

"Just before the storm hit," Anton said as he coughed up another mouthful of salt water. "There was this rogue wave that just suddenly appeared, at least fifteen foot tall, but I didn't see if he caught it."

"Fifteen feet, no wonder your board snapped in half," the surfer said as he looked blankly out to sea.

Anton saw the three figures running down the beach towards them carrying a stretcher. There were two lifeguards and what appeared to be another surfer. He knew he was in no condition to be able to walk back up the beach, and the lifeguard station was probably the best place to wait until they found Johnno. So he didn't argue with them when they placed him on the stretcher, only clutched the remaining half of his surfboard knowing that the other half was still out in the sea, along with his friend.

"We'll find your friend," he remembered one of the lifeguards saying to him above the sound of the rain. "As soon as this storm eases off we'll be able to spot him and go out there and bring him in."

Anton lay back on the stretcher, closed his eyes and the world turned gray.

epilogue

T he next morning broke solemnly over Kings Beach. The warmth of an early autumn day's sun filtered down through a small break in the clouds as it lingered for only a few moments above the horizon. It was one of those quiet mornings where it was easy for Tanya's thoughts to float off to faraway places. As the sun climbed steadily in the sky, long morning shadows stretched across the tables and chairs that Tanya had just finished setting up outside the café and briefly bathed the setting in a golden ray of hope. Then the sun disappeared behind a cloud and the moment was gone.

In front of the café, the sea stretched out like a blanket of blue-gray. The ocean was calm, except for the regular crash of small waves that washed up on shore in fifteen second intervals. Although the sound was normally soothing in the still of the morning, it offered no comfort in the wake of a restless night.

Tanya hadn't heard any news on Johnno's whereabouts since the lifeguards had found his surfboard washed up on shore shortly before nightfall. She'd spent all night in prayer. Her heart torn between the emotions of thanking God that Anton was alive and the dread that choked her in knowing that Johnno was still missing. Tanya had stayed at the hospital with Anton until shortly before midnight. Finally the nurses had convinced her to go home and get some rest. Anton would be free to leave in the morning after they kept him overnight for standard observation. Earlier she had phoned Sebastian. He had rushed to the hospital, only to spend an hour apologizing to the both of them for his emotions sliding out of control yesterday. When they had finally assured him that all was forgiven, he'd insisted on being there early this morning to check Anton out of the hospital once the doctors gave him the all clear on their early morning rounds. Anton's only concern however was for his missing friend.

Somehow in her heart she knew Johnno was alive. Alone, but still floating in the ocean, perhaps miles off shore by now and scared that he may never be found. All she could do was trust God that the lifeguards would find him this morning, as promised, when they resumed their search shortly before daybreak.

Tanya sat down at the same outside table that Anton and Johnno occupied almost every morning. It was less than twenty-four hours since she discovered the two boys huddled around the poem they had pulled from the bottle. Her poem she reminded herself, and instantly hated the negative thoughts that followed. All she had wanted to do was let go of the guilt she had carried in her heart every time another birthday rolled around. It wasn't her fault that her parents died in an auto accident on their way to visit her for her birthday, and she no longer blamed God for taking them away from her. But this was all too much. This had all stemmed from the poem she had hoped would help free her from the past. Only it had made the past seem all too present once more. She caught the tear before it had time to roll down her cheek and breathed deeply. There was still time.

"God where are you when I need you most?" She began praying quietly in the courtyard in front of Mermaids Café. "You have opened my eyes to so much these past few days. But why do the most important lessons in life always cause so much pain? I should have shared the Your Truth with Johnno like I have with others time and time again. Instead of hiding my Faith from him and thinking I was doing the right thing by controlling the feelings I was hiding for him in my heart. I don't know if you allowed the things that people wished for yesterday to happen, or simply put those around me in the path of what was destined to occur anyway. But I do know that we all need Your Grace right now. There is more power and lasting goodness in prayer than there is in making fanciful wishes. Right now Lord I pray that you would return Johnno safely to us all, and that lives may be changed for Your Glory as a result. Please God, I ask this in Jesus name. Amen."

Tanya let the words float softly in the air when she had finished. In her mind she pictured the search and rescue team finding him alive, floating offshore and waving to the rescue helicopter as it swooped by low overhead. Only it bothered her that she had not seen any sign of a helicopter so far this morning. She should at least be able to hear the distant whir of a helicopter flying low overhead, unless...

"Umm, Tanya," a voice softly interrupted her thoughts. Surprised, Tanya turned to see Kim standing quietly by the table.

"Kim, what are you doing here?" She asked, no longer able to find any bitterness within her towards the woman she'd grown so jealous of only yesterday.

"I've just spoken with Jake. He told me everything that happened yesterday. Tanya I'm so sorry, I feel awful for what I said," Kim apologized.

"That's okay," Tanya spoke softly, remembering that Kim's last words to her late yesterday afternoon had been to wish that she couldn't be with John either.

"No it's not," she corrected her. "I should never have said such a horrible thing. I feel like this is my fault, just like the accident on the beach yesterday."

216

"I was the one who wrote the poem and put it in the bottle," Tanya sighed. "If you want someone to blame, then you could probably blame me."

Kim stood silently for a moment, obviously processing this new slice of information.

"I didn't know you wrote the poem," she finally spoke up. "But I did hear you praying out loud before. I hope you didn't mind me listening while I waited for you to finish. But now I really know how you feel about him."

Tanya froze with embarrassment. She had never recalled praying out loud in public before. Had she really said the words out loud while she poured her heart out to God?

"I guess I liked John for all the wrong reasons," Kim continued. "John has a good heart, just like yours. So I hope God answers your prayers. I on the other hand am lucky that the owner has given me another chance at my job."

"Jake has given you your job back?" Tanya finally found the ability to speak again. "What about yesterday and all that money from the beach? I thought you'd left town for good."

"Ah, I already decided to give it back this morning," Kim blushed. "I couldn't sleep last night. Having that much money that I knew wasn't really mine just ate me up with guilt. So I handed it in at the police station on my way to work, anonymously of course. Anyway, Jake said to tell you not to wait on any tables this morning. Just to sit here and wait for any news on when they rescue John."

"Thanks Kim," Tanya sighed, now more confused than ever. "It will be nice to finally leave yesterday behind and start afresh."

"I hope we can still be friends," Kim reached down and hugged her tightly. "And I know you and John will be able to work everything out when he gets back."

"I hope so, but I still haven't heard any news since late last night." She seemed surprised by the open display of affection coming from the girl who in Tanya's mind was the enemy up until a few moments ago.

"They will find him Tanya," Kim assured her. "John is such a strong swimmer. Besides that, I heard your prayer before. I know I'd rather believe that God could answer a prayer than a letter in a bottle could magically grant a wish."

Tanya felt like crying again, but the past twelve hours had drained her of all her tears. So she let the words hang silently for a moment before putting on a brave face to turn and quietly mouth the words, "thank you."

Kim smiled before she turned and disappeared inside the café, leaving Tanya's thoughts to once more return to the rescue helicopter plucking Johnno from the sea.

Somewhere in the parking lot, the silence was interrupted by a vehicle as it pulled into one of the spaces still half buried in a sand drift from yesterday's storm. Tanya barely acknowledged the noise as the doors opened and closed. Her thoughts were far at sea while her eyes strained, searching for any sight of a helicopter patrolling the horizon. So the voice that followed almost caused her to jump in fright.

"Yesterday you said you loved me. Today I need to know if you still feel the same way given that the bottle is probably halfway over the horizon."

Tanya barely had time to turn her head at the sound of the voice before her mouth dropped wide open at the sight of Johnno standing beside her.

"Johnno, you're alive! Thank God you're alive," she leapt to her feet and threw her arms around him. "I've been praying all night long that God would bring you back safely, and he did. He did."

Johnno felt her body pressed against his for the first time. Everything felt new to him. The smell of her hair, her cheek pressed against his, her arms wrapped tightly around him. He knew the answer to his question without needing to hear her say it.

218

"Of course I still do," she finally answered. Tears of joy now welled up inside her as she buried her face into his shoulder. "I just thought I'd lost you before we even began."

Johnno quietly returned her embrace, letting his arms slide gently around the beautiful girl who sobbed quietly into his shoulder.

"When I was out in the ocean, all alone, I remembered what you said yesterday. You know, how a relationship with you could last a lifetime, but a relationship with God could last for eternity."

"You did?" She sniffed back the tears that begged to pour out.

"After I lost my surfboard in the storm and I started to drift further out to sea, I prayed like I haven't prayed since I was twelve years old. I told God that I didn't want to die without experiencing either. Just then the storm clouds parted overhead, bathing the water around me in pure sunlight. A passing fishing trawler caught sight of me and pulled me from the water. It had to be God's doing Tanya. Only the storm had knocked the radio out on the trawler and they couldn't get the word out that I was alive until they made it back to port in the early hours of the morning."

"It's amazing who you meet at the hospital," Anton interrupted. Tanya looked up and noticed that Sebastian and Anton had been standing behind Johnno all along. "We would have phoned, but Johnno wanted to see you in person. Besides, we needed Sebastian to give us a ride once the doctors gave us the all clear. The Kombi was still where we left it in the parking lot yesterday."

"Well you're here now," Tanya sighed as she cuddled back into Johnno's arms, "and we are going to make sure we do this right, starting with mending your relationship with God. We have the rest of our lives to watch our love for each other grow."

Johnno picked Tanya up off her feet and squeezed her tightly, so tightly that she thought she couldn't breathe. When her feet touched the ground again her whole body shook, and then the tears followed. They flowed from deep down inside her, cleansing her heart from years of pain, guilt and sorrow before leaving the pair clinging to each other in a long silent embrace. Only the gentle crashing of waves could be heard on the shoreline. There was no sound of screaming children or crying babies. It was as though the moment was caught in time, lost somewhere in the solitude of an early morning at the beach.

Later that day the gang gathered inside Mermaids Café. Tanya, Johnno, Anton, Sebastian and Kim all crowded in around one of the tables on the upper level.

"I was so glad when I heard they'd found your friend alive and well," Sebastian said to Tanya. "When the nurse woke Anton at three in the morning to tell him the good news, you can only imagine how quickly he wanted the doctors to give him the all clear so that he could go and meet him."

"Look, about Johnno," Tanya interrupted him. "I think I should explain the reason for my actions the other night."

"You don't have to," Sebastian assured her. "I can see how happy the two of you are going to be together. Look it's all water under the bridge now, and I'm sure we'll stay friends for years to come."

"Are you sure?" Tanya questioned him further, sensing there was something else on his mind.

"There is one thing I wanted to mention to you however, and that is I'm putting my house up for sale today. I didn't want you to think I was moving on because of the way things ended with our dinner the other night." Sebastian's words brought the thoughts of the others back from their animated conversation.

"Did I hear you're thinking of moving?" Anton turned to face his friend. "When did you decide this?"

"I know it seems kind of sudden, but it was something you said to me yesterday Anton that made me realize what I should do," Sebastian said before taking a long sip of his cappuccino.

"What did I say?" Anton asked curiously.

"You said you wished I'd make up my own mind about what I want to do in life," Sebastian replied. "So I'm selling my house and heading off to Alaska for a while. I've got it all figured out. By the time I come back they will have finished building the condos where the holiday park is now. I only hope it's not a sore point that I'm planning to pay a deposit on one."

Tanya looked anxiously in Anton's direction for a reaction. There was a brief moment of silence as the words sunk in.

"Good for you dude," he said as the sun began to dip from view in the early evening sky. "I don't know what the future has in store for all of us. A part of me wishes I knew, but I think its best that we somehow learn to enjoy the moments we spend trying to figure it all out."

"Hey look everyone. John is on the evening news," Kim said excitedly as Jake rushed from behind the front counter to turn the volume up on the TV.

"*News tonight of an amazing story of survival following fears that last night's severe weather that lashed the entire stretch of coastline had claimed the life of a local surfer. John Clark, more affectionately known as Johnno to his friends was presumed lost at sea after being reported missing while attempting to surf in treacherous conditions off Kings Beach. Johnno himself was only yesterday regarded as a local hero following the bizarre accident that saw Kings Beach closed off for most of the afternoon. After rescuing the drivers of the vehicles involved in yesterday's accident, it seemed the rescuer became the rescued after a stricken fishing trawler miraculously plucked him from the sea, alone and miles from shore shortly before nightfall. After being unable to venture into the nearest port on account of the heavy seas, and with no radio to advise that the missing surfer had been found, friends and family were forced to wait overnight for any update of the situation. Their prayers were answered shortly before 3 am this morning when the trawler sailed into port. After*

undergoing a routine medical check, Mr Clark was free to leave
the hospital with his close friend Anton Rubinski who also had
been rescued by local lifeguards from yesterday's dangerous
conditions. In a touching conclusion to this near tragedy, both
men shared the winning third place ticket drawn today in their
local lifeguard fundraiser and will take home between them a
brand new moped. Reporting from Kings Beach this has been..."

"How about that huh?" Anton sat quietly as the news sank
in. "We won a moped."

"Ah, that's about all the fame I can handle for a lifetime,"
Johnno laughed as Jake turned the television off. "Besides,
tonight isn't about me. It's about a special someone whose
birthday was ruined yesterday. Now where's that cake?"

On cue the lights of the café went dim and Jake made his way
out of the kitchen with the birthday cake he had prepared
during the day.

"Happy birthday to you, happy birthday to you. Happy
birthday dear Tanya, happy birthday to you."

"I'm sorry I couldn't make your birthday party last night,"
Johnno whispered in Tanya's ear. "But I do hope I get invited to
all of your birthdays from now on."

"Well don't just sit there," Anton joked with her. "Blow out
the candles and make a wish."

CPSIA information can be obtained at www.ICGtesting.com
Printed in the USA
BVOW010711070212

282298BV00001B/168/P